THE SHORT HELLO

For Frances Campbell,
who won the War single-handed:

and in memory of Leonard Maguire, actor and writer,
1924–1997

THE
SHORT HELLO

SUSIE MAGUIRE

Polygon

Polygon
An imprint of Edinburgh University Press Ltd
22 George Square, Edinburgh

Typeset in 11 on 13 pt Linotype Sabon
by Hewer Text Ltd, Edinburgh, and
printed and bound in Great Britain by
Bell & Bain Ltd, Glasgow

A CIP record for this book is available
from the British Library

ISBN 0 7486 6271 5

The Publisher acknowledges subsidy from

THE SCOTTISH ARTS COUNCIL

towards the publication of this volume.

CONTENTS

Sincere thanks to those who encouraged my writing, and equally to those who offered criticisms; to the people who laughed at the right times and the ones who laughed at the wrong times; to the ones who listened and the ones who wouldn't; it all evens out in the end.

Thanks to Polygon; to the Scottish Arts Council; and to The Taxpayer, who has so kindly supported me with tiny sums over many years.

Four of these stories – 'The Day I Met Sean Connery', 'Barry Norman's Tie', 'Aftershave' and 'Incomplete'. – were first broadcast on Radio 4; grateful thanks to David Jackson Young, of BBC Scotland, who originally produced them.

THE DAY I MET SEAN
CONNERY

Nobody believes me. Nobody. They just give me the fish eye, and go 'oh yeah, right, Marina', like I'm some wee kid that has to make up stories. Maybe they're just jealous, though. Maybe they'd never have had the nerve to actually do it? Like my friend Agnes, she goes mental if you mention. Tom Cruise; or Veronica, she'd spend hours pulling her tights straight if there was a single chance in a million of getting close to Kevin Costner. Used to be it was Christian Slater, but Veronica's into older men now. The young ones are pathetic she says, and I've got to agree with her. Pathetic? They're hypothetical! Look at Tommy MacAuley, at her party, the way he stood in the hall smoking with all his stupid pals, and never once danced. See, older men have got past all that, and if you can put up with them being a bit bald or a bit fat, and having no clothes sense whatsoever, they're actually a lot more interesting, really.

Anyway, that's kinda how I feel about Sean. I've always thought he was brilliant, never mind that my mum used to drool over him in *Dr NO* and stuff, that never put me off. See, I think he's really got class – his wife being a painter, a bit of a John Bellany, kinda thing, all elongated and weird, and he seems to be wearing yellow v-necks in all her paintings, like he's just come off the golf course, and she's said 'freeze', or 'gelado' or whatever you say in Spanish. And that's another thing. Him speaking foreign languages. No way some young dipstick from Broxburn is going to take you to a restaurant and speak Spanish or Italian to the waiter. I dunno, just playing golf, and speaking Spanish, and having that deep voice and a great tan, and his really dry, very *very* dry humour, it all adds up, doesn't it? A perfect man.

Anyway, I was at the BBC in Glasgow, well, I went into the shop to get a Delia Smith book for my gran, and you had to go through reception, see? So I was just standing there, behind a couple of messenger guys with these huge Darth Vader helmets, who were flirting with the woman behind the desk – God, mutton dressed as lamb, all puffy sleeves and doo-dahs in her hair. So I sat down, right, they've got this TV, it's always turned to BBC, apparently, except at night, when the staff switch over to watch *Brookside*.

Anyway, it was on Ceefax, just going through these pages of news items, like about what a mess it was in England with all the floods, you know, and how fed up the insurance companies were about these sort of Acts of God, which serves them blooming right. They only really pay you any money when you die, and then what good does it do you?

Anyway, on the Ceefax it said blah blah blah Sean Connery, and I went OOOYAH, and read it quickly before the page changed. It was about him coming to Scotland to do a charity thing, a presentation, and it was going to be filmed by the BBC – today! And I looked around me, just casually, and nobody else had even noticed, they're all standing there in the exact same positions, looking bored, and Sean Connery is about to be in *the same building*! I couldn't believe it. And then I went – hang on, just hang on: what if I got to meet him? So I looked for a sign – you know, Ladies? – and decided I'd better go and look at myself in a mirror to see if the news had changed me, like my hair was standing on end, or my eyes had expanded or something.

Anyway, I went through these doors, and along a blue carpet in a blue corridor. People went by, but no one gave me looks, so I carried on, found the loo, went, and then put on a bit more make-up. I think eye-shadow makes me look like Jodie Foster in *Bugsy Malone*, but Veronica says it's sophisticated and mature, so I bunged on loads. Maybe they'd think I was Claire blooming Grogan, and give me a part in a play.

Anyway, I went back out, and wandered down a few more corridors, looking into offices as I passed – women typing, men talking on the phone. Typical. I found a lift, and went in and pushed a button, and got out one floor up. I turned left and found the cafeteria, which was quite empty, and I felt a bit nervous, but there was loads of really gorgeous-looking food for about 5p, so I had a vegetarian lasagne and salad and a coffee and a Kit-kat, and found a newspaper, and sat and read and nibbled and sipped this dire coffee for about an hour. People kept going past with trays of this and that, amazing what people will eat, eh? Yoghurt and crisps? Is that a well-balanced meal? I bet these people get ulcers and die when they're forty-three, sitting in the dark all day in front of a VDU, eating crisps and yoghurt.

Anyway, four men came and sat down at a table nearby. All of them looked the same, they had big beards, greyish longish hair, denimey sort of shirts, like ZZ Top, but definitely not. They started talking about casting, and production costs, and stuff, so I suppose they must have been Producers or Directors or both. One of them would mention an actor, someone I'd heard of maybe, and the others would all go 'nah, too old, too fat, too young, too London, too Glasgow, his agent's a bitch . . .' They didn't agree about a single thing except that the coffee was weak, and that Scotland had no chance against Holland next Saturday. I was thinking about moving away when one of them said something about Sean. Then another one said, 'yeah, Craig's going to fetch him from the hotel about now, he'll be here for a 2 o'clock meeting', and the others all looked at their watches and sighed and moaned about work they had to catch up on, and they got up and started to leave. Blasé, or what? So I followed them, at least I followed the one who'd said all that about Craig. He trudged down dozens of stairs, and walked for miles and kept saying Hi to people. Eventually he went through this set of doors that said Studio Two, Silence, and all kinds of warnings about not going in if the light was red, but he had, so I followed. It was a huge, massive great place, with loads of people dragging lights around, and tiers of seating, and a big blonde woman wearing earmuff thingmies, standing on a stage area talking to herself – she kept saying, 'no, he's 6'2" and he's *not* wearing the rug' like it was a long-running argument with the Invisible Man.

Anyway, I took a notebook out of my bag, and stood in a dark corner, and tried to look official. The lights kept changing, and the monitors went on and off, and there were bits of old footage of Sean, looking absolutely divine, with this cool sharkskin suit on. And Sean's talking but I can't hear the words, though his voice is in my head going 'Up Perishcope, Up Perischcope', like in *Red October*. Oh God.

Anyway, just as I was looking at my watch and thinking '2.15 where is he', in he came – Sean. Mr Connery. He was dressed sort of casual but expensive, Pringle's best and a cap on his head. I suppose his head would be cold in Scotland, eh, after all the sun in Marbella? There was a wee crowd round him, and I had this brilliant idea that if I just tagged along, maybe no one would notice. So that's exactly what I did. The minute they left the studio, I was on the trail, I'm telling you, it was V. I. blooming Warshawski – without the power dressing.

Anyway, all I could see of Sean was this cap, striding along out in front, with the grey-haired Producer guy I'd followed earlier nattering away at him about auto-cues and stuff. Sean's voice was a low rumble, monosyllabic, actually. He didn't sound very happy. We reached the lift, and Sean and the Producer slipped in, while the rest dithered, because it was obvious they couldn't all fit, but no one wanted to be the odd one out, so eventually the Producer said 'look, chaps and chapesses, meet us up in my office, okay?' and they all turned like sheep to go up the four flights of stairs. But I stuck my foot in the lift door, and smiled and said 'Going Up?' – honestly, I don't know where I got the nerve – and there I was, standing right next to Sean Connery. He was *ginormous*. I could have touched him, I could even have spent hours touching him, if the lift had got stuck, but it didn't. I just had a few minutes to gaze at the middle bits of him out of the corner of my eye, and take in the aftershave, and notice the freckles on the backs of his hands and then the lift stopped. I stood aside, and sort of waved my hand, meaning you go first, but he did that thing with his eyebrows that makes his nostrils flare, and said 'Ladiesh firsht' and I swear to God I nearly melted into a wee heap.

Anyway, I got my legs moving left right left right out of the lift, and then pretended to be really fascinated in this manky painting which had sort of twigs and stuff on it, not Joan Eardley, but some pathetic student rip-off merchant's idea of a winter landscape. I was keeping my ears open, as they went past me down another blue corridor and through a door at the bottom. All I heard was the words tea and make-up. I started to think, what am I doing here? What do I want? If I do get to talk to him, what am I going to say? and stuff like that. I didn't want to go in and ask for his autograph like some silly wee lassie, it had to be something else. Then I had a blinding revelation. Shortbread. He must really miss shortbread, in Marbella. I went pelting down the stairs to the first-floor canteen. I got a tray full of tea, coffee, real milk, sugar, and a huge plate of tartan-wrapped individual bits of shortbread. I carried it very very slowly to the lift, and went back up to the fourth floor, and down the corridor to Sean. I took a deep breath, and knocked on the door. He said 'Come in', and I swear there was a wee lisp there, even on just those two words! So in I went, and he was sitting at a sort of Hollywood-style make-up table, with millions of light bulbs round it, in smart suit trousers and a white shirt, combing his moustache. Our eyes met through the mirror, and I nearly died. He said 'Ah, tea.' 'Or coffee, if you'd rather,' I said. 'BBC coffee is always terrible,' he said, with this wee smile, and I nodded, like I knew what he meant, and I did. I poured him the tea, put the milk and sugar to hand, the teaspoon in the saucer, and pushed the plate of shortbread until it was practically under his chin. 'Bet you've not had this for a wee while,' I said. 'Go on, put some in your pocket for later, I always get peckish when I'm trying to go to sleep and have to sneak a biscuit.' I could hardly look at him, like I didn't want to actually see him, in case he disappeared. But he sort of laughed, and I did look, and he has these incredible eyes, dead crinkly, and deep, and it's like taking some powerful illegal substance or something, I just felt a big whooosh – like: I Have Met Sean Connery and I Can Do Anything. Incredible. Magnetism. (I bet he could've made money as a hypnotist, if the film career hadn't panned out.)

Anyway, that was very nearly the last word I had with him, because right then the door opened and another tea-tray appeared. No shortbread. There was this big silence when the woman carrying it saw me, and then she just smiled and opened her mouth and shut it a few times, and finally inclined her head like she was conceding defeat, and backed out. My face must have told the story because Sean gave me a funny look. Then *he* poured *me* a cup of tea.

Anyway, I had to tell him, eventually. I just couldn't keep up the facade, you know. But he was very nice. He could've yelled, or phoned security or locked me in a cupboard, but he just looked at me, just – looked. And then he said 'why?' And I went 'Why? Why, Sean? Don't you realise by now that there are millions of women who'll never meet anyone as good-looking as you, or as funny, that we're all going to have to settle for less? You're unique.' I probably went on a bit. I told him about myself, and my last boyfriend, and how we'd broken up, and how I didn't know if I should go to college. He raised the eyebrows and smiled like he was trying not to laugh. I didn't mind. It was great just having him there to talk to like a normal person. And he gave me lots of good advice, which I'm not going to pass on. He told me his golf handicap, and what he thought about Kevin Costner. I daren't tell Veronica. Finally, there was another knock on the door, and the grey-haired guy stuck his head through and went 'AAh AAh' and walked in sort of stiffly, rubbing his hands. And that's when I knew my time was up, so I stuck my hand out, and Sean stood up, and shook it, and said 'it was nice talking to you . . .' and I said 'Marina, Marina McLoughlin, very pleasant talking to you also, Sean.' Then he turned to the man, who had this sickly sort of grin on his puss and said 'Kenneth?' and I waved, and backed out of the door. And as soon as my legs un-wobbled, I made a run for it.

Anyway, that's the story about how I met Sean Connery. Veronica and Agnes aren't having it. I nearly phoned my ex-boyfriend, but you know, something stopped me, and I think it was the big whooosh I'd got off Sean. I thought no, I don't have to settle for less. Stuff Michael and his mountain bike and his bloody Gold Bier. I'm worth better.

POETRY IN MOTION

Big sticks. Feathery sticks, all sloping, standing straight but with their arms hanging down, long long arms down to the ground. Green so dark it looks black, sun so white it hurts, coming through the feathers of the trees. Millions and thousands of trees, all the same, but some taller and some nearer and some when the car got close enough had red in the bark and they looked so rough it would hurt your hands. Too tall to climb.

– Dad? Dad? Dad? Dad?

– Yeah?

– What trees are those?

– They're pine trees, honey. You know the cones we found in Granma's back yard? That's how these trees started, little pine cones.

Dad talks about the trees, how old they are, and everyone else listens and joins in, but the light comes bursting in the rear window and Mickey turns his head back to the road streaming behind him.

Red car, red car, blue car, white car, green truck with yellow sides, red car, red truck with no top. His lips move quietly as he counts, three, four, five . . . Pink road. Grey patches on the pink road, tarmac. The smell of it back home, the City, a hot day. Mummy holding his hand. The traffic lights go red and the green man appears. Hurry, Mickey, says Mummy. She tugs on his hand and they walk past the big smiley bumpers on the car fronts, shiny, dirty, walk-walk-walk on to the pavement. Hurrying to school to meet Trudie, then slowly home, past the computer shop Mummy likes, past the wine shop, the newspaper shop with the really old man, the flower shop, the baker's shop. Cakes. She said he could choose. Apple tart or chocolate slice. Apple tart he remembers, with raisins, and the pastry a bit wet.

– Dad? Dad? Dad?

– What, Mickey?

Rosa answers, not Dad. Dad is practically deaf. Mickey has heard Rosa say this, so it makes sense when he calls Dad that Rosa hears him first, but sometimes she pretends she doesn't hear him, sometimes she just looks at Dad, or touches his knee. He always looks at her when she does that. Sometimes Rosa touches Mickey's knees too, and it makes him kick and laugh, she squeezes too hard.

– Dad, are we nearly there yet?

– Nearly, just a little while more, says Rosa.

– Another twenty clicks, maybe, before we turn off – we have to go right to the top of the hill and down the other side before we get to the river, honey . . .

Dad's voice changes when he talks to Rosa, sort of quiet and warm, but laughing. He calls her honey, too. She calls him darling. Darling Dave. Mickey can't see from the back, but he bets she has her hand on his knee.

– Rosa, I'm hungry.

– Well, it won't be long until we stop and have our picnic. It'll be all the nicer if we eat by the river.

Peanut-butter and strawberry-jam sandwiches, cheese sandwiches, juice. Dad and Rosa will eat chicken legs. Mickey will not look. He will hold his nose when they open the box. Dad says chickens are dumb birds, dumb egg machines. Mummy gave him an egg once. It was crumbly, and she put it on toast with butter and ketchup and cut it small.

Mickey straightens his legs as much as he can on the pile of coats in the back of the car. You're gonna sit where the dogs go, Kevin had said. Trudie had said Shut UP! and pushed him and they had a fight. Mickey rolls over and kneels and presses his nose against the glass. His breath makes a fog, and he rubs his nose against the glass even more to wipe it off before Dad shouts that he can't see a goddamn thing. The man in the car behind waves. He has a moustache. His wife is fat. She has a cigarette in her hand. Mickey pulls the coats into a different arrangement, like Uncle Frank's big yellow dogs do with their blankets, sits down again.

> Blue car, dark-blue car, green car.
> Pink road, grey road, pink road.
> Green trees, white sky, grey clouds.

– Dad, what does it mean, Allegheny? Trudie is asking.

– It's the name for the place, honey. For the forest and the mountains. Actually, I think it's the name of the people who lived here.

– Indians?

– Mm-hm.

– Don't you mean *Native Americans*, darling. . . ? Rosa laughs. Her voice is not like Dad's, more like Mummy's. But Mummy has dark hair.

Allegheny. Mickey holds the word in his mouth and makes a shape with it. Al – la – gay – ni. Allegheny. The wheels make a sound on the tarmac which is like Ala – gayni. The man behind puts on his blinkers and overtakes their car. His wife throws the cigarette out of the window on to the road. Allegheny road.

> Allegheny road. Allegheny cars,
> Allegheny cars, Allegheny hills,
> Allegheny hills, Allegheny river,
> Allegheny river, Allegheny people,
> Allegheny people, Allegheny trees,
> Allegheny trees, Allegheny trucks,
> Allegheny trucks, Allegheny birds,
> Allegheny birds, Allegheny forest,
> Allegheny forest . . .

– Dad, Mickey's making a poem!

– Shh, Kevin, let's hear it, says Rosa. She turns herself round in the seat, her hair dragging behind her like a big red curtain, and calls, Tell us your poem, Mickey mouse . . .

> He smiles and starts again – Allegheny road,
> Allegheny road,
> Allegheny cars, Allegheny cars,
> Allegheny hills, Allegheny hills,
> Allegheny river . . .

– Rosa, Honey, will you write it down, there's a pen in my rucksack . . .

– That's really good, Mickey, says Rosa, can you

remember it and say it again?
– I don't know . . .
– Go on, Mickey, says Trudie.

Mickey focuses his eyes on the road, pink and grey, the sun flashing through the long dark trees, the cars whooshing past on the other side of the road, the smoke coming from under their car, under him, watches it vanish into the air.

> Al – a – gay – ni smoke, Allegheny smoke,
> Allegheny cars, Allegheny cars,
> Allegheny picnic, Allegheny picnic,
> Allegheny trees, Allegheny trees . . .

BATHTIME

T he sound of Hugh's unpacking in the bedroom reached Amy's ears despite the hot water thundering into the tub. He hummed, too, something new. Sounded happy. She bent to test the water, twisted the cold tap open another fraction, and started pulling off her clothes. She brushed her teeth, spat, rinsed, peered at her gums in the mirror. Long in the tooth was just an antiquated expression until you saw it happening in your own mouth. Was she old? Older. Grey in her hair now. Mercifully the mirror was misting with steam and she was too short to see more than her face and neck. She turned from the image, the thought, and shut off the taps.

– Bath's ready she called, I'm getting in, okay?

She lowered herself slowly into the water, with an habitual groan of pleasure, and sat still, legs folded, eyes closed, waiting for Hugh to join her.

He was singing now, the same tune, with words like 'gotta get' and 'baby baby baby' and 'your love'. He tipped the last bundle of clothes out of the suitcase on to the bed, and held each garment to his nose to test for freshness. One by one, t-shirts and underpants and socks and jeans were tossed to the floor. He paused to unwrap a green notebook from some thick tartan flannel, slid it up on top of the bookcase by the stack of sketch pads and project journals. He started to unbutton his work-shirt, then changed his mind, took down the notebook, and sat on the edge of the bed, flicking through the densely covered pages.

Amy lay back in water hot enough to make her skin tingle and thought about the past week, the latest in a succession of such weeks, broken only by Hugh's brief return home at weekends. Meals cooked for one, eaten in front of the t.v., taking a hot-water bottle to bed and reading till her eyes stung, mornings sedate and ordered without Hugh's usual hurried starts and half-eaten breakfasts. Work, solitude, thinking time. Good but not good. She replayed their latest mid-week phone call.

– Amy, hi, it's me.

– Hi, sweetie, did you get my card?

– Yes, thanks, nice –

– Did the meeting go okay?

– Not bad, spent two hours on site waiting for the guys to show up, some misunderstanding at their end, but they liked the piece – Ian doesn't foresee any problems, so . . . heigh ho . . .

– Great! You sound tired, though . . .

– Yeah I am, need to eat, need to lie down – how are you?

– Fine – sort of – look, I'm sorry about all the hysteria,

Monday morning – you know? It just – I hate it when you look so happy to be leaving. Quite unflattering! But I got lots of work done – wait till you see . . . hey, let's go out on Saturday night? See a film or something?

– Sounds good – I have to go, the money's running low.

– I'll call you back?

– Ah . . . doesn't accept incoming calls . . .

– See you Friday then –

– About ten probably, maybe later . . . oh, Amy? Will you tape that Art thing tonight for me?

– Video's already set.

– Okay, bye then –

– Bye . . .

The sound of his voice had been reassuring. His presence in the house, humming away softly in the bedroom, was more so. Her eyes teared, and she pushed the wet sponge against them, hard, and sat up. Her chest was thumping and she felt dizzy. Might be the heat, though the water was cooling, warmth drawn away into the corridor through the open door. She called again – it's getting cold! and Hugh replied – be right there! but she knew his habits, and resigned herself to a longer wait. She poured a little bergamot oil into the water and ran some more hot, swirling it round with her hands. She forced herself to visualise an orange grove, sun and the smell of hot earth and blossoms, to forget her anxiety about Hugh, and the distance between them.

Hugh noticed the passing of time differently from other people. An hour might be the time it took Amy to write three letters and create a risotto, but for him it was only long enough to choose a brush, maybe sharpen a couple of chisels. Two hours might suffice for preparing a canvas, six for making a single drawing. Reading took longer, too; for pleasure he liked to roll the words around in his mind and visualise every one of them separately and then together, as they made up a sentence, like a row of coloured marbles. He struggled with time. There was never enough of it to spend on traffic tickets, bills, bank statements, so he left them until Amy's panic forced him to react with ill-humour. Eating, especially popcorn, and driving, particularly when late – and he was often late – were occupations where minutes and seconds flew too fast for him. Now, browsing through his green notebook absorbed him to the point where only the slow summer dusk made him conscious of the passage of time. That and another plaintive call from siren Amy.

With Hugh settled behind her, his legs spread out touching the tap end, knees bent like the arms of a recliner, Amy could adopt her favourite bath-time position, leaning back against his chest, the top of her head fitting under his chin, their arms wrapped together. Safety Position, Hugh had once called it. Waves of affection swept through her at the memory. The internal commentator, who thought like her big sister Liz, fluted in her irritating way 'See, everything's fine as long as you keep calm and cheerful.' Amy understood, really, that everything wasn't fine. Nothing had been fine for a long time, unnoticed until Hugh's new commission, his repeated departures gradually eroding her feeling of safety. Bath-sharing was traditionally an opportunity for them to talk, to be close. Hugh sighed deeply. Amy knew enough to read his sighs, and that one was not purely fatigue. She had made a pact with herself not to chatter, above all not to question him about what he did down there, during the days they were apart. She planned to leave spaces big enough for him to speak first, but keeping silent was harder than she had imagined. The absence of conversation seemed ominous to her, and she wondered if he was unaware of it, or if he was daring her to start talking, interrupting his peace, giving him the excuse to start an argument, withdraw from her even further. A small ember of resentment glowed next to the warmth of her grateful affection.

Unaware of his coded sighs, Hugh's thoughts were of stone. Warm sandstone, pink-gold, curved where he cut and chiselled it, and granite, resistant, solid, cold. Slate, smooth and blue, grey York paving, cement, turf, sand, steel and new, tungsten-tipped chisels. His hands were callousing nicely. His back hurt, and his knees, where he'd crouched, when he tensed against the recoil from his blows. The shapes were there, every half-day another form emerging. Keeping focused on the sculpture stopped him from thinking about anything else, specifically what to do about the changes to be made in his life, what to do about Amy.

She began to cry, so softly at first that only the change in her breathing gave her away. She knew why she was crying, knew about tension and release, hoped Hugh would respond by comforting her as he used to, knew absolutely that he would not if he thought she expected it. She sat forward, reaching for the cold face-cloth, and held it to her eyes and nose, but soon her body began to shake in the helpless rhythm of grief. Another sigh escaped Hugh, this time followed by an – Oh, Amy. . . – full of resignation and regret which put miles between them more rapidly than Hugh's weekly train journeys south.

– 'Wait' said her sister's voice, 'Wait, you're jumping to conclusions, you're projecting.' But Amy hung her head, ashamed to be crying, apologetic and furious, unable to stop unless stopped. The whole evening was yet another assault course she had failed, would always fail.

Hugh thought about his lack of response. It surprised him to feel so little at her distress. More strongly came the illumination that he was too tired to care about her any more, and bored with the repetitious scenes, Amy sobbing and shouting when he went away, angry and scared, and still tearful, needy and reproachful, when he came back. He looked at her hair, clamped to the top of her head with a cheap pink comb, examined her back, noticed the way her spine bent, and thought of his sculpture. He ran a finger down the bumpy vertebrae, then reached out both hands to her shoulders and rested them there. Her skin was marble to the eye but warm and soft, and he experienced a flash of fucking her bent over the bath on some previous occasion, weeks, years before.

Amy felt her tears slow as her need to speak increased.

– Please – don't be angry with me . . . The words petered out. She felt his heat as he came closer to lean his head against her left shoulder, the bristles pressing against her neck and chin. His arms came round her again, his hands lay loosely on her thighs. She leaned into him a little. She breathed deeply, a shudder, then almost a sigh, and felt a bit of fear go out with her exhalation. Back in safety position.

– You're unhappy. She nodded, her ear brushing up and down against his eye socket. His simple statement of fact was a relief, an acceptance, maybe they could go on from there. Her face puckered, but she breathed deeply again and caught it. Her hands moved over his, tiny in comparison, and pressed gently. He turned his over and they locked fingers, church and steeple.

– Okay, he said. Okay. And after a while – This water's getting cold.

Amy got out first, wrapped herself in a towel, and went to the basin to wash her face. Hugh pulled the plug and stood up in the bath, shaking the water out of his hair. Stretching, he made a friendly sort of yawning growl. Amy looked quickly at him to gauge his mood. Hugh climbed out of the tub, stood yawning again, rubbing his hands across his face and into his hair, his mouth relaxed, curved up just enough to presage a smile. Amy picked his towel off the rail and touched it to his chest. She turned away to open the door and let some cool air aid the process of drying her skin, bent to pick up her discarded clothing. Her towel dropped around her feet as she gathered the bundle for washing and stretched for her slippers under the chair.

Amy wondered, as Hugh gripped her hips, if the animal part of her had led her to the submissive position by instinct, the way she often gave way to Hugh's demands because they seemed more powerful than her own. Pliant. Willing. Not how she felt inside, but a position to adopt in times of fear, because fear gave off a scent to the stronger animal, and sex was a way to diffuse danger. The danger of her need threatening his need. This is how it was between them now, mostly. Her wrists hurt, hands shock-absorbers flat against the tiles. She was not in her body, but observing their fusion as an illustration from some grubby piece of fiction, distanced from the rawness. She closed her eyes, then, and allowed her body to soften and rock with Hugh's motion.

He shifted his stance a little, ignoring the twinge from his knees and lower back, and felt his body arc like a bow as the moment peaked. Fragments of imagery sparkled kaleidoscopically in the descent. The one which made him open his eyes again was the repeating pattern of ridges in the outer kernel of a split nectarine, the way it would feel to run his fingers over that, carved in stone. He wanted to write it down, draw it, make it.

He bent to kiss her on the neck, cupped his hands around her breasts, his touchstones, and disengaged gently as she moved in response. The aftermath of sex had always reminded Amy of lunar modules docking and undocking clumsily in slow motion, but this time she could only see herself still foolishly bent and vulnerable, wanting more, always wanting more, unhappy. Unhappy. He had said it, she now realised, as though saying it meant something new, as if a decision had been reached.

Hugh wiped himself clean with the damp edge of his towel. He squeezed toothpaste on to his brush, the need for sleep advancing, his thoughts fluttering around in sentinel mode; Amy, quietly wiping between her legs, back arced again, the sculpture, in sunlight and then glowing, as it would be now, under moonlight, curves and silhouettes, shadows thrown against the grass. Amy, her hand on his buttock as she reached past for something, his notebook, his next train journey, music on the Walkman as he chipped and cut at the stone slabs. Relief. Amy's acceptance when he had expected major drama. Sleep, sleep, sleep.

Hugh put one arm round her, pecked her cheek.

– I'm beat, he said. He moved slowly towards the bedroom. Amy sat on the edge of the bath and debated painting her toenails. She rubbed some hand cream into the skin of her heels, washed her hands, combed her hair. She took her clothes and the damp towels into the kitchen, shoved them in the washer-drier with a dose of detergent and turned it on. The remains of supper had congealed in the casserole dish, so she threw out the lumps, left the dish in the sink to soak, and turned out the light.

Hugh lay flat on his back, fighting off sleep. He knew there was something he had meant to say, explain, confirm, leaving, changing, becoming happier – gone now. Amy slid into bed softly beside him and clicked off the lamp. Hugh's breath came in little huffing noises, a prelude to snoring, so Amy pushed against him to turn him over and he finally complied with a moan. She lay behind him, wanting to reach out and hold him, to tease his skin with her teeth and nails, to rouse him to another sexual encounter, but not feeling good about it. She was sore and tired, and still she wanted him, but vindictively, only for him to want her, to not have had enough of her, physically if nothing else. As a punishment, a quid pro quo. What kind of mentality had she fallen into that allowed her to think and feel and behave like this, she wondered. The tears came back but she made them stop this time by conjuring a cool blue light around her head in which she was entire and contained and serene. She breathed in through her nose and out through her mouth, tilting her neck to relax it, letting her jaw drop. She extended the blue light to her toes and up her legs to her knees, and on, but it was hard work, kept changing to a darker colour, a purplish red she associated with her dissatisfaction. She gave up. Although her limbs were heavy she felt restless. She lay with her eyes open, watching the shapes on the ceiling flicker according to the whims of the streetlight's damaged tube, counting the hours until she could take out her diaphragm.

GYROMANCY: A FABLE

Once upon a time there was a man and a woman.

The man lived in a grand wooden house on stilts, perched high on a mountain side, the better to see out of his windows the state of the world as a whole, which observation he noted daily in an immense leather-bound book with a jewelled silver clasp.

The woman was the owner of a stall at which townspeople and travellers could buy fables. Every morning she set out, wrapped in blankets to withstand the poor climate, and sold piecemeal her neatly penned parables to all who wanted them, coming home at night to take up her quill once more in the light of a single candle.

Both the man and the woman lived quite unaware of each other's existence. The man knew that women existed, and the woman knew that men existed; they saw them every day in the course of their occupations. The woman noted men's chins and eyes, the smell of their clothes and the colour of their hands as they fumbled with coins to pay her. The man saw women in groups of colour and noise, like exotic parrakeets chattering on the wing, flurrying beneath his window. But they did not see each other. Their own worlds sufficed, and so time passed.

But one night while they slept the strangers met. In her dream, the woman set out upon the path which led to her usual place of work, though she was carrying none of her wares. In his dream, the man rose from his comfortable chair at the window and walked down the mountain side.

She found her path deflected by new walls, closed gates, crowds of people who seemed not to recognise her without her basket of words. He discovered a series of steps cut into the mountain, strewn with leaves and dangerous chips of rock, which made his descent risky but swift. She walked rapidly, marvelling at the appearance of houses, shops, avenues she had never explored, being in her usual routine always burdened and dutiful. His feet took all in their stride, though he never looked down, for his eyes were fixed on the new evidence of natural life about him; the animals, birds and insects he could see now in more detail than ever before.

She sighed as she saw how others lived, with families and laughter and comfort about them, in such contrast to her own. He sighed as he noticed how, cheek by jowl, the creatures managed to survive, the spiders and the flies, the cats and the mice, the goats and the lynx.

She came, in her dream, to a wide grassy space with a carved stone bench, upon which she stretched herself to look up at the sky. He came, in his dream, to the same grassy space and, seeing the bench occupied, sat to one side, by a clump of scented narcissi.

He looked with suspicion upon the blooms, and said to himself – these are not real. I am dreaming.

She looked at the sky and said to herself – how wonderful it would be to float as high as those clouds.

He looked at the woman and said to himself – she is looking in the wrong direction if she wants to understand the world.

She noticed the man and said to herself – how uncomfortable he looks down there among the nettles on the damp ground.

She beckoned to him to share the bench with her. The man dusted himself down and sat on the edge of the stone, where he could run his fingers across the carvings of mythical creatures which adorned the weathered face of the bench. The woman examined his face and found it strange. Even in her dream-state she thought she recognised this man. The man looked back at her with equal curiosity, certain that he too had encountered this woman somewhere before.

They looked at each other until the day became dusk. They did not speak, because dreams do not truly contain speech, but communicated by the use of some better language. As dusk turned to dark, and they could no longer see, each felt the dream drawing to a close, and moved closer, hand seeking hand across the still-warm stone. Just as their fingers found each other in a clasp of friendship, just as their dreams faded, they recognised each other. She was Woman. He was Man. They had always known each other; they had never truly been apart.

From that time on, they met often in dreams, upon the carved stone bench in that grassy place where the unseasonal narcissi perfumed the air.

Gyromancy – a kind of divination performed by walking around in a circle or ring until one fell from dizziness, and so was in a fit state to see visions, speak in tongues, etc. (*Brewers Dictionary of Phrase and Fable*)

A Night In

I'm mixing a packet of white cheese sauce when the phone goes, and I have to put it on speaker, but it's Dave upstairs wanting a jam session, so I tell him I'll call him back. Fucking scald myself on the kettle trying to pour the bastarding water in and when I've finished cursing and hopping, I put my whole arm under the cold tap for about five minutes. When it comes out it's still sore, but maybe because it's freezing now. I rub some Vaseline on it and put my shirt on and button the cuffs, which looks mental but what can you do? Finally I get the sodding cheese sauce on the sodding pasta and chuck some black pepper on and it goes in the oven at 6.23, so I reckon that's going to give us twenty-five minutes more or less to talk about my music centre and her dress and get a glass of wine down us before the lasagna's brown and toasty on top. That's if she's on time. That's if she comes.

I met her in the pub down by the train station. I never go there, but this one night last week I had a real thirst, and I was just walking back from the gym and I started day-dreaming about cold lager. Hallucinating the taste of it. Cold lager and a bag of cheese and onion crisps, talk about a way to undo all your hard work, and I'd spent an hour, maybe an hour and twenty tops, working out, really sweating for Scotland, but fuck it, sometimes you've got to just treat yourself. Women do it all the time; you hear them talking about how they've had such a bad week or a row with some mate and they go for retail therapy and all that. Okay, it's their money, and I can't complain about the result if it catches my eye, and it does, but they spend it on the wrong stuff. I've never met a woman yet who couldn't waste a whole day trying on shoes and then spend £80 a time on the first pair she tried on, but they'll walk right by the places that sell a decent widescreen t.v. Every single woman I know has a tiny wee portable, absolutely bloody useless, might as well be a radio. It's not that they don't want one, don't know the difference. It's like they're waiting to get it given to them by some mug. Meet a guy, sleep with him, get engaged, and then lie back and wait for the hardware to just fall out the sky at their feet.

Anyway, last week. Never been in it before. I sat at the bar and asked for a Beck's. Nice old place, not been done up or themed, but not too scabby. It must have looked okay outside anyway, because suddenly there's all these girls in through the door. Place was quiet, like, but in they

come, there's five of them, all a bit giggly. They all take
seats, stools, up at the bar, and start ordering glasses of
wine and Bacardi and Coke and stuff. Two old guys
sitting at the back of the room drink up and leave, taking
their time about it, and then apart from a wee guy in the
corner on his own reading the *News*, and the barman,
that's us.

The barman's a bit dozy, so he has to get them to go one
at a time with the different drinks they want. It's not the
kind of place where they keep much of the stuff women like
in fancy bars. There's no call for peppermint syrup, and
maraschino cherries, you know what I mean? But they've
got mixers. So, they all get their drinks and they notice one
by one that they're the only females in the place. They're
talking quite loud, all up and confident. The place starts to
smell less like a bar and more like a make-up counter, five
different makes of shampoo, five different perfumes, five
different body odours. It's nice, but kind of druggy almost,
the sudden laughing and their smell. I'm watching it all in
the mirror, though I've clocked them along the bar too.
One of them is pretty bossy, she's got dark hair and she's
like the head girl, definitely top banana. The more I listen
the more I realise they've all been doing some sort of
evening class together, an all-woman thing. I give the
barman a nod for another Beck's and sit there, just listening
to these voices. How can they all talk at once and still listen
to each other? It amazes me. And they've all got plenty to
say.

They've made a kind of circle of their bar stools. The
bossy lassie, she's giving it some about men, no surprise
there, but she doesn't have the sense to lower her voice, not
even a wee bit. Educated voice. She's saying they'll have to
have a girls' night out properly some time, and another one
chips in that they should all go out for dinner, and then a
third one says why don't you come to my house, and all

bring something, and we'll do it that way. Then the dark-haired bossy one says, but you'll have to send your boyfriend out for the night, and some of the others laugh. And she says, on the other hand, give him an apron and get him to make the dinner. The one whose boyfriend they're laughing about says no, God no, Graham's a terrible cook. Can't even break an egg. Piss-poor co-ordination then, one of them says, aaw, poor you. Yeah, well if he's like that with eggs, another one says, letting it tail off, and they all laugh again. Men are crap with their hands, the bolshy one says, especially in the dark. Give them a screwdriver and they're away, but they've never actually worked out what to do with a woman's bits. It was the way she said it. Bits. I hate that. Like they have no reverence for their own bodies, you know? Fucking say fucking vagina! You know? And on top of that stuff about men, generalising, it really pissed me off. My fingers are tapping by this time. The barman's polishing away at his bloody bar, keeping stumm, no solidarity there. I put my bottle down just a bit sharp, and one or two heads turn. I look over at them. There's a bit of nervous laughter, and the bolshy cow, she says oops, we're being a bit sexist, girls, and pulls this face, like ooh, the things we'd say if you weren't there, laddie.

So I get up, and take my bottle and I go over and stand next to them. They all go pretty quiet. The bolshy woman, I'm standing behind her, she has to turn her head if she wants to see me but she won't because that would make her look stupid, which is fine with me. Just to needle them I say, I hope you 'ladies' are having a good evening? Yes, thank you, say a couple of them. So far, one of them adds.

I can't believe it, they're all fucking terrified. Of me. It's not like I'm a hard man, but I've scared the shit out of them. But I don't want to back off. I've heard this bollocks a million times and I don't know, maybe it's the two Beck's on an empty stomach, but I feel like I have to say something or I'll burst. I have to dare them or something. I just can't sit there taking it.

I look at each of their faces. There's lines you can tell on a woman's face if she's a right snippy wee bitch, and only a couple of them have it, both brunettes. Most of them drop their eyes quite quickly. I won't deny I enjoyed the power of that. The one I liked, though, she holds my eye for a while, she has red-brown sort of hair, just dead straight, not very long, on to her shoulders. Wee fringe. Short nails. Not frightened, curious. I stop looking at her, because I decide she's different, and I like her. And then I say, maybe you 'ladies' are right. Maybe some men are stupid fucks, and some men are clumsy bastards, that may be so. But every one of us is as different as every one of you. So please. Please, don't tar us all with the same brush. Please, don't come in here from your art class or whatever it is and start with the labels. Because you don't know me from Adam. I like women. I am good with my hands. I cook and clean up after myself. I am not a fucking Neanderthal, okay? Their faces, the ones I can see, go blank. I'm speaking really quiet, gentle, nothing offensive, just saying it like the truth it is. I say, I have feelings. I can feel hurt by people who make cutting comments. I'm just sitting here having a drink after a long day and I would like a little respect paid to my right to do that in peace without names being called. So if you don't mind, 'ladies' – I say it again – 'ladies', just to make my point. And then I walk back to my seat, and sit on it, and take another swig, and look at them in the mirror. I don't look down or away. I meet their gaze. Their gazes. No, not gazes, little flickers, little darts like neon tetras in a tank.

The head girl gives me a quick smirk, like aye, right, okay, point taken, but that's where I draw the line, no surrender you bullying bastard. The others are mainly whispering, almost anyway. The one I liked the look of has her back to me. She pushes her stool back, stands up, puts her glass down. She turns round and walks towards me. Jesus! I think she's going to say something and I half turn, but she walks right by me to the toilet. And I'm thinking oh, fuck me! Because I nearly spoke to her first and I have no idea what would have come out of my mouth. Maybe a 'hiya', some stupid thing.

The others all drink up quick enough. When their friend comes back out they hurry her up to finish hers, and they all leave. I suppose I've made them leave. All the adrenalin's making me feel dizzy, like I've lifted too much weight. I put my Beck's back to my mouth. I've got a hollow feeling in my chest, because I think, that's it, I can't talk to her now.

Just when I'm thinking that, she comes back in, on her own. She walks up to me and looks at me. Her face is dead serious, a bit pink-cheeked, maybe from the cold, maybe from her drink. Her ears too, pink lobes with these little crescent moons on them, silver. A blue scarf tucked into the neck of her green suede coat. She says, I apologise for Lorraine and the rest of them. You're right, sexism works both ways. We forget that.

I'm so surprised I don't know how to come back. I must be staring at her. She looks down at her feet, and then looks at me again, and then pulls her bag on her shoulder a bit more, and says, I just wanted you to know. And before I can work out what I want to say, I've said it, can I have your number? She looks at her feet again. What is it with women that they can't just look at you? She's looking up and away again, like there's something really fascinating over by the door to the toilets. I say to the barman, hey pal, can I get a pen?, and he gives me one, so I write my number down on a beer mat, and give her the pen and the mat, and she writes her number down too, and then tears it in half, snaps it really, and gives me her number. And she's got mine. And then she smiles and says goodnight, and leaves.

I get home and chuck my gym gear in the wash and zap a pizza and watch the telly. I've got the half beer mat on the coffee table, her writing in blue ball point down the side, no name, and I think how will I know if it's her? What if she lives in a flat with lots of girls, or what if her mum answers? Or a man? But before I can get that stuff stuck in my head, I pick up the phone and I dial it. A woman picks up and I know it's her, even just hello, out of breath like she's just got in.

I say, hello, eh, this is James, I'm the guy with the other half of your Woodpecker Cider bar mat. And she goes oh, that was fast, I'm just in the door. Can you hold on a sec?

I go, sure. Then I can hear her shutting a door, and rustling like she's taking off her coat, the green suede one, and dropping her blue scarf, and a whoosh like she's sitting down close to the handset, and she picks it up again and says, back again. I go, what are you called, then, or shall I just think of you as the mystery woman? She laughs, and says something, enigma I think, and I say eh? catching it a bit late, and she says it's Sandy. And I say okay, hello Sandy. And then there's a wee pause. Her breathing, me breathing. I say, look I really appreciate you speaking to me, because you must have thought I was totally out of order, and I really don't know why I did that, and she interrupts me, yes you do. Another wee pause. It's okay, she says. We've done that bit, now what? The directness of it.

This is all happening so fast I've lost the plot entirely, sitting there with my mouth open, trying to find the way to respond, saying eh . . . and laughing, and she laughs too.

Nice laugh. I've got the paper open to the t.v. page and I see there's a food programme on, well, I've missed it, but it gives me an idea, so I ask her if she wants to go for a meal. And I remember what they were saying about men not being any good with their hands, and I say, come round to my place and I'll cook for you.

I can practically hear her going through the options, is he being straight with me or does he just want to jump me, is he a weirdo, what if I get stuck with this guy, but it's like a test. Either she'll trust me or she won't. I give her my address and suggest a day and a time, and I say, listen. I'll cook for two, you come if you want to, if not, no problem. And she goes, okay. And just before we sign off I say, Sandy? See that group of women, were you all doing an art class, or what? And she says, well, actually, no. Self-defence. See you then, James. And puts the phone down. So maybe she's a karate expert, or she does kick boxing, but more like she's just screaming and hitting cushions with a baseball bat, fat lot of fucking use in a real situation, but all credit to her for making an effort.

So I'm sitting waiting for her to arrive. If she doesn't come I'll give Dave a ring, and tell him to bring his sax down and we'll have a blow. But if she does? Salad ready in the fridge, coffee beans in the grinder, bottle of red open by the gas fire. I haven't changed the sheets, because I don't expect anything, and I'll be quite happy to walk her home or to the bus stop or call her a taxi or whatever. This is flying-by-the-arse-of-the-trousers time.

And I've been thinking about the sexism bit. It does go both ways. That's something I've been waiting a long time to hear a woman say, and I hope we can talk about that sort of thing, if she comes. It's twenty to now. I'm turning the gas down on the lasagna, just to stop the top getting burned too much. My arm hurts still, a bit red too, but I don't want to roll my sleeve up, and I don't want it buttoned down either, so I take my shirt off and swop it for a sweatshirt, pale grey with a zip at the neck, and I've got my head pushing through it when the doorbell rings. If that's Dave, I'll fucking kill him.

High Heels

From head to toe her skin was smooth and lightly bronzed, more sheen than colour, a faint summer stain. On her feet, old-fashioned tan and white court shoes clopped as she ran on the bare boards from bedroom to closet to living room, clutching bundled silk and crumpled crepe, laughing, flirting with herself in the mirror. She pressed a flowered print dress against her chest, bent her right leg at the knee, swivelled, flounced, flung the garment on to an easy chair and teetered away again into the hall, leather soles skidding a little on the varnish. The voice floating behind her sang 'It's Too Darn Hot', off key but in tempo with the screech of hangers on rails, and his heart turned over with tenderness and a little sadness.

He recognised that this was rare for her, a mood he might never see again, a temporary high induced by sunshine and circumstance, while he himself was passive, reflective. The wardrobe review had been a sudden inspiration on returning from holiday, in the thrill of seeing her normally pale skin turn into gold under a 60 Watt bulb, and the discovery that Greek food and frequent swimming had eased off a few surplus pounds. It was not her habit to be naked in broad daylight, but the instinct was, he felt, to be encouraged. Her body looked different, contours refined by the tanning, and the two inch heels altered her proportions, her stance, lifted her usually modest walk into a new category of femininity. The sadness he felt was unusual, and he dismissed it, but the wave of tenderness came of a familiar and vertiginous desire to seize her and demand a sexual response, to capture her in this moment of self-absorption and confidence, when he felt so comparatively weak. Unusually, he merely stood, leaning against the mantelpiece, watching the performance, acknowledging with surprise that he could choose to hold back. It made him ache all the more to mould himself into her when he knew his presence was almost irrelevant, that he was only another mirror in which she sought and found her own answers.

Looking at herself in the pier-glass, her ankles slimmed by the solid shape of the 1950s shoes, her calves and thighs taut, stomach pulled in, hands on waist, breasts and nipples tight in the cool of her six o'clock kitchen, hair tossed across shoulders, chin up – she hardly recognised herself. For a long slow moment she was assaulted by mental images of another woman, herself as a different person, different inside as well as out, happier, sexier, better at life. How could the addition of a couple of tones of beige give her the illusion of confidence? Why did skirts that met at the waist make her day? How long would it last?

She became aware again, felt his gaze. He observed her silently, with a twist to his lips, an incipient smile that might have been a comment bitten back. What he made of this whim she didn't know but, while she had admired his objectivity and restraint, now she felt awkward, and yearned to be not distant, unobserved, compelled by the weight of his body. Her temporary confidence had brought her to a peak of sensitivity to the sensuality in her own body. She felt weak, standing there in a blue silk shirt that skimmed her hips, catching the way her eyes looked so bright and blue in her brown face. It made her float, to imagine being held so closely that there was no room for thought, for individuality, for consideration. No room for yes or no or please or don't or there. She longed for it, and feared it, saluting the duality of her nature, understanding also that he was bound to her as yet only physically, that he did not, might never, perceive the second, third, fourth levels of battlements in her mind, hadn't even remarked upon the narrow tower at her centre, with the candle burning in the window. In letting down her hair, she was only offering him a ladder to her exterior, and the hidden passages remained unexplored.

He uncrossed his legs, took a step to the chair, lifted a short red linen jacket from its hanger, and proffered it. She threw off the shirt, slid into the jacket, the lining cold for a second, buttoned it up, five gold shells, smoothed the collar, folded the cuffs. The fabric glowed, and the last glint in the evening sky flew into her skin and hair, as she pivoted before the glass. The sunlight created a flaming bush between her thighs, matching the softer, longer ropes of hair curling down her neck. Unconscious of the effect, she turned from the mirror and saw it, saw in his eyes and face that emotion he didn't like to call sadness. He wants something he doesn't know and will never have, she thought, and immediately responded to that loss as if she was comforting herself for the same reason, taking his head between her hands and resting it on her shoulder in a gesture that said – Let me take away the sins of the world, let me renew you, let me offer you shelter, is this what you want to hear? She stretched up on her toes in the two-tone shoes, feeling heat as his arms wrapped around her, his warm hands flexing against her goosebump skin.

He bowed towards her, his face into the crook of her neck, absorbing her through all his senses, and felt the sadness ebb, and his weakness changed into strength, as her strength become tender. Then he found it easy to say that he loved her.

A BROWN STUDY

A fictional episode in the true life of Scottish Comedian Arnold Brown

The sun rose that morning on a day like any other. A day for breakfast. Croissants to be eaten, papers to be scanned, mail to be read . . . ah, but the first post wasn't due until 9am. Those once-familiar morning routines, all changed now. His heart bucked at memories of the Hampstead years, but he had a quick word with himself about regrets, in the spirit of Frank Sinatra, and turned swiftly to practicalities. He would go out for papers before the postman could knock even once.

The customary ablutions completed, he slipped into his usual weekday wardrobe of black cotton chinos, dark plaid shirt, corduroy jacket and suede lace-ups. He pushed the still luxuriant hair back from his craggy face, and stepped out on to the streets of NW10.

The quality of international patisserie is variable throughout London. Moving house required a period of research to discover the best source of morning pastries and afternoon fancies, bagels, baguettes, brownies. His heart leapt this time in hungry anticipation, as he walked the streets of Kensal Green in imaginative parody of a bloodhound. Nose and eyes soon led him to the Bonjour Bakery, where he was served by a young Frenchwoman who called him Sir, a gesture of civility which surprised him. Perhaps it was the corduroy jacket, as worn by the late François Truffaut? Perhaps it was his confident French pronunciation of 'pains aux raisins'? Whichever, the 'Sir' put a spring in his step as he paced homeward, collecting both *Guardian* and *Independent* on the way.

In the kitchen, the habitual hunt for teaspoons was averted by the kindness of his beloved, Liz, who had placed a dozen apostles in a Gretna Green mug by the kettle, bless her heart. He took the cafetière through to the dining nook, sought fig preserves, opened his paper, poured the coffee, and took his first bite of pastry. Flaky, moist, buttery, just a tad under-baked – $7\frac{1}{2}$ out of 10. His gourmet deliberations were interrupted by the prompt arrival of the postman with a large padded packet for which he was asked to sign.

Despite the news of Richard Branson's most recent balloon fiasco ('Dick In Another Fine Pickle' – a touch tabloid for the *Guardian*) and the amusing assertions by the *Independent*'s t.v. columnist that Reeves and Mortimer were just Eric and Ernie on speed, Arnold was too distracted to enjoy his breakfast, diverted from a second croissant and the remains of his mocha-java by a compulsion to open the mysterious package. With a glance at the clock, and a sigh, he abandoned the last crumbs and dregs of the repast and conveyed the parcel into his study.

The study was brown. On purpose. Brown paper on the walls, brown chair, brown cushion cover. He liked the joke, even if it was more a boxroom than a study. Space for reference books on a wall of shelving, two filing cabinets, a portable radio and a table large enough to call a desk, when he mentioned the room to fans – e.g. 'Thank you so much for the paperclip sculpture/book of Scottish jokes/snaps of your cousin's barmitzvah, which will take pride of place above my desk . . .'

Arnold wrapped a Burberry scarf about his neck, and placed a battered tweed deerstalker on his head, flaps down, to combat the draught from the skylight, and reached for the ornamental dagger he used as a letter knife. The puffy envelope contained a plump yellow cardboard folder marked GOB, and a covering letter, clumsily typed.

```
Dear Arnold,
   Please find enclosed as much as I could
photocopy of the financial papers relat-
ing to a business in deep dog dirt. I refer
of course to the comedy club GOB. I know
you've never been booked there, Arnold,
so you might be a bit peeved, and I agree
it's a liberty, but let me just say that I
believe you to be a kind and decent man,
and I'm sending these accounts to you in
your capacity as a private financial con-
sultant, rather than your public persona
as a comic genius. No flattery, I'm being
honest. I've got a lot of time for you,
mate. No one does one-liners like you
since Chic popped his clogs. But I di-
gress.
   You probably don't know about the busi-
```

ness arrangements for GOB, but they're complicated. You'll have heard it's owned by Bill Blythe, but behind him there's quite a few of us working stand-ups who know more about comedy than cash, so Bill is just the flash jacket and twirly bow tie, if you follow.

For obvious reasons we can't go public about putting our money where our mouths are -- or were -- now most have us have hit the t.v. Not like Robin Williams and his yoga centre. It doesn't play well this side of the Atlantic, making a profit, not very clever when you might still do the Tunnel Club with new material of a Friday.

Anyway, there's six of us and Bill makes seven. He's supposed to deal with the money. We had a little Sunday lunch meeting without him last week and compared notes, and four of us think he's dodgy. The other two are on the fence. (Har har.) I shouldn't say any more, let us know what you think when you've shuffled through this lot.

We've gone dutch on the dosh, so there's a postal order stapled to this for 600 quid to cover your investigation. Don't ask me how to explain it to HM Government come April -- you're the accountant! When -- if -- you've got something to tell us, do a gag about kippers at the Jongleurs Anniversary thing, and we'll make contact.

Cheers mate,
GOBs Anonymous.

Carefully verifying the cash amount on the postal order, Arnold gently replaced the letter on the desk. He leaned back in his seat, allowing his eyes to roam the cork-tiled area above his desk, while he mused on the fate which had brought this matter to him. For several minutes he sat quietly, the only movements a subtle smile on his lips, a raising and lowering of his eyebrows, a gentle back and forth twiddling of thumbs. Finally, he pulled his spectacles higher on to his nose, sat forward and opened the GOB file.

* * *

The following morning found Arnold back in his brown study, perusing the most recent tax-assessment guidelines to be had from the Inland Revenue's local enquiry centre. Many things had changed since his early days in accountancy, such as the introduction of decimal coinage, but two and two were still obliged by logic to make four. Unless he was very much mistaken, GOBs Anonymous were right to be suspicious. It was not so much that Bill Blythe had been particularly devious, but that the average comedian hadn't the mental arithmetic to keep abreast of cash flow, lulled all too easily by smooth-talking agents and managers into casual acceptance of remittance slips without paying scrupulous attention to the large percentages or the small print. Arnold thanked God, and more particularly his old primary-school teacher, Horace 'Whinny' McWheen, for instilling in him the fundamental principles of multiplication, subtraction and long division, in the golden age when personal calculators were still the stuff of science fiction.

By 3.30pm, just thirty hours after receiving the file, Arnold was satisfied that he had Mr Blythe down cold. No contented smile played about his lips, however. Pinpointing the embezzlement in the GOB accounts had been relatively simple. Writing a kipper joke was going to be tough.

Arnold took to the streets again, this time forsaking delicatessens for the local fishmonger, where, under the pretence of looking for a supply of gefilte fish balls, he stealthily examined a pair of kippers. He didn't like the look of them. Smoked haddock had passed his lips on occasion in Scottish B & Bs while touring from Carlisle to Cowdenbeath, but the kippered herring was alien to his experience.

Kippers were, to his mind, a taste-test of patriotism, as English as P. G. Wodehouse, as Churchill or Arthur Askey. He could imagine any of them eating kippers, but what was funny about that? Dead men eating dead fish. And why did they always come in pairs? Was there a Siamese-twin joke in there? Possibly, but he couldn't think of one just at that moment, and took scant consolation from an apricot tart at the Bonjour, before making his way home to watch *Countdown* and prepare supper.

The sun came up as usual on the morning of the Jongleurs Anniversary party. Arnold too was up bright and early to exchange pleasantries with Natalie at the Bonjour bakery. (Her pronunciation of 'Arnold' was getting better, and so were her croissants.) But he ate breakfast without his customary relish, anxious to closet himself in the study and polish the new gags for the evening's event. A kipper joke still eluded him, and it stung his professional pride to think of being beaten by a fish in front of his peers.

The anniversary party was a private function, attended by many television and radio producers, as well as numerous performers on the comedy circuit, some of them household names now, thanks to sit-coms and talk-shows and movie cameos. Arnold didn't envy any of them that burden – he'd been there, done that, worn the novelty y-fronts, while most of the current stand-ups were still in Pampers. He knew the perils of the life; faulty tele-prompters, alcoholic floor managers, vindictive warm-up men, audiences bussed in from geriatric facilities . . . or was that just Kilmarnock? In any case, if comedy really was the new rock 'n' roll those smart-mouthed journalists kept insisting it was, Arnold had no wish to become an object of derision like Jagger, a come-back kid like Bowie. For a moment he wondered if his own favourite popster, Bryan Ferry, was still cool and still crooning, then dragged his mind back to the ordeal of the night ahead.

A Brown Study

The club, when he got there, was packed. Arnold accepted a glass of champagne, nodded to a few media drones, then stood quietly by the bar and observed the room. There was Sean Hughes talking to Hattie Hayridge, Paul Merton haranguing Angus Deayton, Tony Allen rolling his eyes at Andy Greenhalgh over the heads of Saunders and French, and Arthur Smith, Jo Brand and Mark Thomas arguing about the running order. All the old familiar faces. A malcontent with a tenner's worth of Semtex could wipe out two generations of comedy talent in a single explosion were he so inclined, but, as Harry Hill was saying to the assembled crowd on a quite different topic, what was the likelihood of that happening, eh? Harry finished his set and Phil Jupitus ambled up to the mike.

Though outwardly calm, Arnold was in fact jumping with nerves. Part of his mind was still flicking through an internal lexicon for anecdotes, wry asides, or words to rhyme with kipper, while another part was occupied with assessing the possible identities of GOBs Anonymous. Eddie Izzard gave him a kiss in passing, was he one of the six? There was Charlie Higson, exchanging baby-food recipes with Arabella Weir, both of them waving hello, either of them were candidates; and when Mark Lamaar passed by with an unusually cordial sneer, Arnold regarded his trademark broad silk tie with eyebrow raised in mute enquiry. But Mark moved on to sit with Matt Lucas, and Arnold remained puzzled.

Something was coming to him at last, something about kippers. It slithered around at the back of his mind, refusing to approach the tip of his tongue, but he knew that with a bit of luck it would be there when he needed it. Everyone was doing a strict five minute set, and Arnold's time was fast approaching. He moved closer to the stage, catching the eye of Lee Hurst, compèring the 11 till 12 slot clad in a fluffy yellow fleece and sweating buckets.

And then Arnold was on. With the mike in his hand his mind focused sharply, and the routine snapped out like knicker elastic, brain to lips, inducing the narcotic effect of 'flying by seat of pants' that makes stand-up so special. Doing it for an audience of fellow stand-ups was like a trust game, like falling on to a sea of supportive hands, knowing that even your enemies in the business had to give you respect. Tonight, Arnold felt he deserved every bit of it. His timing was faultless, his famous catch phrase still had legs, and when he came to the new gags he gave them topspin.

During a moment of applause he took a swift look at the faces in front of him. There sat Bill Blythe a few tables back, smoking a cigar, next to Morwenna Banks in a tight pink dress. There was Armando Iannuci, like a little mafioso in pinstripes, and further left, towards the toilets, Ardal O'Hanlon chewing on what looked like a gigantic sausage roll.

Sausages were another thing Arnold had never found tempting in the culinary line. Sausages made from pork put him in mind of the Jewish dietary laws, and that somehow connected to kippers, and gefilte fish, and suddenly, yes, YES! – not kippers, but Kippur, Yom Kippur, the day of Atonement. The final joke coalesced, tingled through his larynx, formed itself in his inimitable voice and hung out there like a disco mirror ball, dazzling the crowd. They loved it. He took his bows, and came off to rapturous applause. And why not?

A few minutes later, Arnold made his way to the gents. He chose the cubicle at the far end, and was in full flow when he heard somebody enter the neighbouring stall. There followed the usual sound effects, zip, Niagara falls, clunky handle and short flush, and then a rustling sound. Arnold looked down. A note had been passed under the partition. Having completed his own business, he sat down and read it.

> Dear Arnold,
>   You were brilliant tonight, and I hope your Yom Kippur joke meant what I think it did?

Arnold took out his medium-tipped Papermate and wrote –

> Dear GOB,
>   Thanks. Yes, Bill is fishy all right. It's all in the paperwork, any trained eye could spot it. Look at his business allowances, clothes, daily subsistence, etc. What are you going to do?

He pushed it back. After a short wait, the paper returned.

> I said all along, Arnold will sort it, he's one of us. You're a star, Sherlock. We can handle it from here. You'll have gathered maths isn't a strong point, obviously, but Intimidation and Ridicule are just two of our middle names. We'll be in touch.

Arnold heard the anonymous GOB leave the cubicle and the door to the club swung open and closed before he could scrawl 'you're welcome' in reply. He tore the note into confetti and flushed it, then went back out to drink a final glass of well-earned champagne.

It was a couple of weeks before the postman knocked a second time at Arnold's door. Once again, Arnold took the registered package into his study, got comfortable in his scarf and deerstalker under the skylight, and wielded the silver dagger over a jiffy-bag. As he had guessed, it contained another poorly typed letter, and a smaller envelope. The letter read:

```
Dear Arnold,
   In the next couple of days you should get
a call from Margie; she's the new manager
who's handling bookings for GOBs. We'd be
really chuffed if you'd pencil in some Sa-
turday nights, or Sundays, at your conve-
nience -- har har. No seriously, hope you
can come and do some gigs for us -- and keep
that kipper joke in, won't you?
   Regards,
   GOBS Anon.
```

The accompanying envelope was addressed to Sherlock Brown, Esquire. It contained a slim bundle of used twenties and a clipping from *Private Eye*, featuring a photograph of Bill Blythe smiling inanely. The columnist sympathised with Blythe over an unfortunate incident culminating in a fall down a flight of stairs in his own comedy venue, in which both legs were broken, painfully, in several places. This lamentable accident had not, the writer suggested, been caused by Bill Blythe's habit of laughing all the way to the bank, but by tripping over the price-tag attached to his hand-sewn brogues. Regular GOB comedians were said to be very concerned. Several of them had generously supplied the hospitalised club owner with his favourite delicacies, including the finest kippers money could buy.

3.30

Anne answers the door in her apron, a parody of 1930s *Good Housekeeping*, cheeks smudged with flour, lipstick perfect.

    – Hello! Come in and give me a hug.

    – Sorry I'm a bit late . . .

    – No no, perfect timing, I've just put the scones in the oven . . . just dump your coat on the chair. Do you want to help me make tea? Earl Grey or Assam? What kind of jam? Peach?

    Fussing. A warmth touches Fiona's face, and her eyes blur, but she smiles and follows Anne into the kitchen.

– Have a seat while I tidy up and tell me what you've been doing. How's work?

Anne's busy hands replace flour in the pantry, sponge down the marble slab, scrub the rolling pin and place it to dry in the dish-rack. Fiona twists her pink velvet scarf around the back of a kitchen chair, answering slowly.

– Nothing much to tell. I'm a bit tired of it all, honestly. Sometimes I think I'd give anything for a change, and then there's a little upheaval – and then I hate change, you know? Yesterday they suddenly replaced all the office chairs, which is good, so many people complain of back problems, but incredibly disruptive timing, right in the middle of a Thursday morning. Drop everything! You know, management versus the workers instead of for them. My boss James is still being a pain. Anyway, I'm due a few days off so I think I'll take them in a lump and sleep for a week. . . .

Fiona is talking on automatic, her interest engaged more by the comforting sight of domestic paraphernalia than the petty difficulties of office life. To her left, the French windows are ajar, and a warm leafy smell mingles with the toasting flour in the oven. Against the yellow walls, framed posters and blue and white plates make an endlessly intriguing pattern, and the mosaic of Victorian tiles in the hearth are a warm patchwork quilt around the display of healthy cactus plants in blue pots.

– How's the flat, how are the renovations going?

– Oh God! I don't want to think about it, there's so much mess, so much to do, I just wish I hadn't started.

– You said yourself you wouldn't have been happy living in a little magnolia-coloured box.

– Maybe I was wrong. Maybe sterile would be restful.

– Try it in one room, white everything, a peaceful space with no distractions?

– Yeah. Maybe.

Anne's hands caress each other briskly under the tap.

She dries them on a striped tea-towel, and reaches for the kettle.

– Five minutes, I should think. Shall we have it in the garden?

– Mmm. That would be nice.

Anne sits opposite Fiona at the kitchen table. She tucks a strand of hair behind Fiona's ear first on one side, then the other. Fiona frowns and shakes her hair loose again. Anne arches her brows with a smile. Fiona traps the quick hands before they can do more, and looks at them, short nailed, practical, not as smooth as her own but strong and warm and dry. For the first time their eyes meet properly and they both hold the look. Fiona drops her gaze back to the tableaux of hands before the kettle starts to whistle.

* * *

From the kitchen doors, the garden appears small, contained within high walls, but the cinder path leads back around shrubs, an apple tree and tall ornamental grasses, meandering down to a paved area with an unexpected tiny white-painted chalet and verandah, some two hundred yards from the house. The wood is warm under their legs as they sit on the steps, the remains of afternoon tea before them on a tray. Fiona rolls up her sleeves and tilts her head back as a cloud permits sunlight to reach her directly for the first time in days. Anne regards Fiona with a smile.

– Such lovely white skin you have.

– Pale and uninteresting.

– No. On the contrary.

– Have you noticed how magazines are full of articles on the dangers of skin cancer but stuffed with pictures of glossy brown skin? Very young and unharmed skin. They ought to have some that's wrinkly, some scars.

Fiona's eyes are shut, slightly scrunched against the whiteness of the sunlight. Her hair falls behind her almost to the top step of the verandah. Watching Fiona bask,

Anne's eyes are thoughtful, attentive, her body relaxed.

– Talking of scars. . . .

– Mmm?

Fiona sits forward now, shoulders hunched, head resting on hands, then more comfortably against her arms, folded across her knees, so that her speech is lightly muffled.

– Did I tell you about the time in Madrid? When I was at University?

– No. Tell me now. I'd like to hear it.

Fiona starts to recount an episode of personal history, her voice light at first, growing flatter and harder. She talks for almost ten minutes before the emotions build into tears. When she cries she look away, until Anne gently reaches for her. Within a few moments, Fiona lies curled across the other woman's lap, sheltered by the presence of a soft bosom. Her hands grip the older woman's hips, Anne can feel the shaking through her pelvis, and against her chest. The uncovered memories stain Anne's slate-grey shirt to black. She strokes Fiona's back and hair, and hums a lullaby. Her eyes follow the bees as they go about their business, a solitary ant discovering the dish of jam on the tea tray, the young cat from next door stalking a leaf in the perennial border.

After a while, Fiona sits up and blows her nose. The vertical lines in her face are accentuated by crying, her pale skin is flushed.

– I feel ugly.

– You don't look ugly.

Anne reaches for the now damp hair above Fiona's ear, and curls it back. This time Fiona permits the intimacy.

– You don't hate me and think I'm awful?

– No. I do not hate you or think you're awful.

– Was I wrong, to behave like that, to let that happen?

– What do you think?

– I don't know. I keep seeing different sides to it. . . .

– Maybe you always will. But you have to choose a side, and it should be your own side, don't you think? Back yourself up?

– I suppose so.

– That's still in the middle, Fiona.

– Yes, then.

– You did the right thing?

– I did the best I could do in the circumstances.

– Good. Remember that.

Fiona's face, still heavy with emotion, gives a flicker of a smile. She rubs at her eyes and nose with a sleeve, flicks her hair back.

– I need to wash my face.

– I'll take the tray in.

In the lavatory Fiona soaks a hand-towel in cold water and presses it against her eyes and cheeks. She stares for a long time into the mirror. The she lets the cold tap run across her wrists, a habit she picked up from her mother in childhood. She dries her face and hands, applies lipstick and fresh mascara, combs her hair, drapes the hand-towel over the radiator. When she comes out into the hall she's aware of the sound of dish-washing in the kitchen, and remembers her scarf, still wound round the chair back. Next time.

Picking her coat off the chair, she digs into the pockets to find the usual Friday envelope and lays it on top of the marble washstand which serves as an internal letter-box at Anne's house. Then she turns the latch on the Yale and goes into the street.

In her sunny kitchen Anne scrapes the last smear of peach jam out of its pot with a spoon and licks it. Still softly humming the lullaby, she washes the container and puts it in the recycling bin. When the front door clicks shut, she walks through the hall to collect the envelope, taking it to her study where she puts Fiona's cheque into her wallet. The accompanying note makes her smile. Opening her diary she makes a note for the following Friday: '3.30pm Fiona, muffins?'

Upstairs, Anne drops her soiled shirt into the laundry basket, kicks off her shoes, and stretches out across the cool blue bedspread. She tugs a pillow from under the cover, and wraps her arms around it, turning on to her side to face a dressing table, bare apart from a family portrait: a much younger Anne, smiling up at a tall, blond-haired man, and between them a small boy clutching a stuffed rabbit. The happy faces contain nothing but love.

Particle Theory

– Were you faking that?
– What?
– Were you? Faking?
– No.
– Were you, really?
– No!
– I'm just asking, that's all.
– You don't 'just ask' if someone is faking orgasm when you're in a relationship and you've just made love! Christ!
Em sits up indignantly.
– Well, it sounded different.

– It's always supposed to sound the same?

– Well, you know . . . there are little noises that you make that you didn't make this time.

Em rolls her eyes and glares, and says,

– How long have we been doing this?

– Doing what?

– Four months it must be . . .

– Actually, I haven't been counting!

– Well let's, then – we met in September, two days after I moved house. Four months. And in that time I have supposedly provided you with a pattern by which you can judge the levels of my orgasmic joys?

– Look, I didn't mean it to sound as if I was judging anything, it just seemed different somehow.

– Different how?

– I don't know, exactly, just not the same!

– Yeah – no triple-axle toe-looping, right?

Em scrabbles for a cigarette and lights up furiously. She punches the pillows.

– Look, I don't know why I asked, I'm sorry.

– Why would you even think about it?

– I don't know. Oh crap. I do. It was that story you told me.

– What?

– You remember, come on, about the time you were with what's her face, Mary something. You told me about it ages ago.

– Wait, I told you I had a friend called Mary Clark, and I haven't seen her for years. So?

– Yeah, Mary, your best friend at college, so; what happened on the night of her birthday when you felt sorry for her because she'd drunk enough gin to tell you how she'd always fancied you and how lonely she was, and you said she could sleep over with you? Hm?

Em stubs out the cigarette, folds her arms.

– Yes, I remember now.

– You told me this maybe the second night we slept together. We laughed about it.

– Yeah, okay, I remember.

– You said there was a lot of fumbling around and how odd it was, like the bodies didn't fit, and how she told you she loved you, and how you felt it was only fair to fake an orgasm and fake falling asleep after that, to avoid the embarrassment of it all.

Em lights another cigarette.

– And this has been preying on your mind for four months?

– Not every second.

– Ha fucking ha. Well, I'm not going to apologise for it, if that's what you're looking for, it was years ago. And anyway, so what?

– Nothing! So nothing! It just stuck in my mind, that's all, and sometimes I get this image of you . . . faking it. And I wonder how I'm supposed to know.

– You're not supposed to know! You're supposed to trust me! I mean what is the point in all this if you don't trust the person you're humping?

– I do! I do trust you . . . I just have that image in my mind and sometimes I look at your face and I listen to you and I have a split-second of a doubt, that's all. You don't have to freak out. Fuck's sake!

– You're the one who's freaking out! You're the one who's suddenly got all suspicious – I think you should apologise.

– Huh, why should I apologise?

– Look. Apologise, or just leave. Your choice.

– How did we get here? What is going on here? I can't believe you're behaving like this!! It's just one stupid little question . . .

– Yeah, and I've answered it, and now you should shut up and apologise.

– Right! Okay, I apologise for asking you a question, all right?

– Fine.

Em rearranges the sheets around her waist.

– And?

– And what?

– And . . .?

– Fuck! *And* I won't ask you again.

– And you won't look at me all the time to see if you can spot me being dishonest or some crap.

– Yes, no, I won't.

Em's face relaxes.

– Good. Right. Move over.

– Oh what now?!

– Close your eyes. Go on.

– What are you doing?

– Well, I'm blindfolding you, aren't I?

– Oh.

– Comfy?

– Now what?

– Ssh. Now I'm going to see if you can have an orgasm when someone's watching your every move.

– Oh . . .

– Of course . . . you could always fake it.

– Aaaaw. . . .

Tangerines for
Christmas

With every ounce of energy she has left, Anna slowly, carefully, slides a hotel envelope from a shelf under the bedside table, and starts to draw on it, in blue biro, the hindquarters of a cow. First the line of its back and tail, the silly tassel on the end, then the line of its belly down into the chunky upper leg, the hock and hoof. Then, with intentional exaggeration, a bulging udder. Anna's drawing begins to resemble a Damien Hirst sketch, half a cow floating in space. She adds spurts from the teats, taking the whole thing into a new, cartoon category. She debates the wisdom of giving the cow Freisian characteristics and decides against it. Too European. Beneath the distended udder she draws a jug, and below that in large capital letters, L-A-I-T. Lait.

She adds an arrow pointing from the jug to the right of the cow's tail. She scrawls a teapot, two heaped teaspoons, and a jar on which she writes the words THE ANGLAIS. Then a traditional kettle, with steam rising from the spout, and a circular arrow connecting the kettle, teapot and tea together. Finally, tiring rapidly, she writes their room number, and the words, SIL VOUS PLAIT, underlined, with three exclamation marks. That will have to do. Her head aches, her joints ache, her eyes ache, and the room spins whenever she moves her neck, but at last her stomach is quiet. She places the envelope by the phone, next to her watch, passport, and handful of dirhams, and gently lies back against the pillow. After the room has stopped whirling, she turns on her side, away from the window. An arm's length away, her sister lies with the sheet pulled up to her ears, so that only part of her face and short brown hair are visible. Her sister Pig, christened Caroline, a name she loathes. Pig's skin looks a greyish green next to the clean starched sheet and, before she loses consciousness again, it occurs to Anna that her own complexion must also resemble that of a Marsh Wiggle. She lets go, slides under, and in her feverish dreams, she and Pig wander the land of Narnia. They look for clues and hide from giants. They stagger hand in hand through cold snow following a pair of webbed feet. In their dreams, the blizzard hides everything from view. In reality, night falls in North Africa almost as dramatically as the snow in Narnia, and both Anna and Pig sleep through the arrival of dusk.

When Pig wakes it is slowly, her lips gummy as a baby's, mouth dry and tongue coated. When she opens her eyes, the ceiling and part of the wall in her immediate vision are bathed in a beautiful purple glow. She flexes her arms and wiggles her toes. Her ears gradually filter information to her brain, and she analyses the situation. In bed. Traffic on wet pavements. No, cobbles. Very small cars with lawnmower engines. Mopeds? Lots of people talking, walking, arguing. The purple light means it's dark outside. What time is it? Where am I?

Pig turns her head to view the window, and beyond it the dingy, plastered building across the street from their room. Just visible is the bottom of a broken blue and red neon sign declaring something which might be café, if she could read it. She remembers it. She deciphers the sounds as both a loud t.v. set and voices speaking Arabic, passionate conversation which, floating through the open door on the same warm air that carries the scent of hot oil and fried onions, brings comprehension. Edinburgh to London to Barçelona to Seville to Tangier. The Hotel Mamora, in the heart of the Mystic Medina. Room 9. Christmas Eve. She remembers Anna's plea for a hot Christmas, a brown Christmas, her delight in Seville until the torrential rain, her suggestion that North Africa would be the perfect alternative to tradition. She replays the journey by boat from Algeçiras, the struggle at the docks, the hunt for a room, and she remembers the taste of their fatal last meal.

Pig pulls herself up against the pillows and glances at her sister, still sleeping, mouth open and drooling against the sheet. This time yesterday they never wanted to eat again. Now, for Pig, the waft of onions is appealing, her saliva not just a by-product of nausea but a sign of returning health. Pig gets out of bed and closes one of the shutters, cutting the purple projection in half. She smells herself under the arms. She sips water. She counts the money in her wallet. She pulls on her trousers and shoes.

One hour later, Anna wakes to the sound of Pig's voice. In French, she is explaining to a small boy that they would like some tea. Thé anglais. The boy stands between the two beds, grinning and nodding. Anna struggles onto one elbow, and reaches for the precious cow envelope. She holds it out towards the boy, but Pig intercepts it. Pig frowns. Just give it to him, says Anna, her voice cross and weak and squeaky. No, says Pig, I've explained. He knows about thé anglais. The boy's smile gets bigger at the word, and he nods again and says 'thé', oui, 'thé'. Just give him the drawing, Anna repeats. He doesn't need to see a drawing of how to make tea, replies Pig, indignant on behalf of this child, this tiny person who speaks two words of French, this total stranger who has aroused her liberal world-traveller complex. Anna gives an exasperated sigh. Pig takes a few coins from the bedside table and gives them to the boy. He pockets them and leaves the room, his eyes lingering on the two women as he closes the door carefully behind him. They hear his feet pounding down the corridor at a run.

Anna sits up slowly, groaning, her stomach muscles hurting more than anything else now. Her head aches less, but her insides feel as if they have been scoured with a steel brush. Anna walks with the gait of an octogenarian towards the tiny cubicle in which the toilet, sink, bidet and shower nestle on a damp grey-tiled floor. She sighs with relief at the new roll of toilet paper, the empty bowl, the clean sink. Pig deserves credit. Good Pig. Thank you, she says.

Pig follows Anna, and proceeds to brush her teeth with bottled water while Anna uses the bidet. I went out, says Pig. Got some more water, some soft loo-roll, painkillers, got some of those glucose tablets. Nice chemist in the souk. Brush, gargle, spit. You must be feeling much better, says Anna. I'm actually hungry, says Pig, how are you? Finally empty, I think. Just want tea. Real, proper tea with milk and sugar. Well, that's what you're going to get, says Pig, with a very slight edge to her voice. Anna isn't up to the sort of argument they would normally have about this sort of thing, about Pig being always right when abroad.

She is barely decent again when there is the knock at the door, and Pig opens it to let in the room-service infant. She takes the tray from him, and he hovers in the doorway. Anna stops brushing her hair and looks at him. Under her serious scrutiny he smiles nervously and quickly shuts the door. That young man thinks we're barking mad, says Anna. Barking mad old women who ought to be married and bringing up babies. No he doesn't! You always say stuff like that! He's just curious, Pig responds.

Anna shrugs fractionally and shuffles to the edge of the bed where she examines the contents of the tray. I don't see any milk, she says, in as inoffensive a tone as she can manage. Pig ignores the comment, continues to fold dirty clothing into a plastic carrier bag. Finally she sits on the edge of her own bed, avoiding Anna's reproachful gaze. Pig lifts the lid of the small tin teapot. The surface of the liquid is a rich creamy toffee brown, and on it float two red and yellow paper labels attached to two drowned tea bags made by Lipton's of London.

That looks absolutely disgusting, says Anna, but Pig pours out two cups of the mixture and passes one to her sister. Anna sniffs it. She unwraps cubed sugar and drops two cubes into her cup, and then stirs it for as long as she can pretend the sugar needs help dissolving. Pig waits for her to finish. They look at each other as they each take their first sip. The milk is long-life, boiled, perhaps even condensed, and the tea is strong and bitter, even with the sugar. Anna sticks out her tongue and crosses her eyes. Pig flares her nostrils, then laughs, her uncontrollable face-splitting laugh, and splutters into her tea cup. Anna produces a sound that is even more bovine than she had hoped for, a long, low, droning moo, and Pig is helpless, half recumbent on the bed, her stomach quivering, the tea cup precarious in her grip. Silly cow, she says, when she can breathe and articulate. Anna has finished her cup and pours herself another. More tepid cow juice, vicar? she says, perking her pinkie at a jaunty angle. Pig slurps down her dregs and proffers the cup, her hand still shaking along with the rest of her, from the release of laughter and the avoidance of disagreement. Hmm, that's better. We should play a game, she says. Charades, maybe. Okay, you go first then, says Anna, inching her way back to lean against the bedhead.

She sips her tea slowly this time, letting it soak into the sugarcube on her teaspoon, as she watches Pig stand smoking a cigarette in the corner by the window. Humphrey Bogart, she guesses. No, says Pig, I haven't started yet. Well get on with it, says Anna. Hoity toity, replies Pig with a smirk, madam must be feeling better. I'll give you madam in a minute, says her sister. Right. Pig draws in her chin, purses her lips, and waggles her elbows. Anna is puzzled. A flying duck, she guesses. A wet hen. A man playing two sets of bagpipes. Harry Lauder. A man with a big arse, I don't know, a trombone player . . . But Pig is shaking her head. No, says Pig, I was being you. What! says Anna. When you're bossy, says Pig, repeating the actions and frowning. They both laugh. Bollocks! says Anna, my turn.

Pig lies on her elbow on her bed and watches as Anna gets up, lights an imaginary cigarette, and walks a few paces up and down the room with an exaggerated bobbing motion, keeping her right eyebrow slightly elevated, a yearning, saintly expression on her face. Pig frowns. Come on, says Anna. It's easy. Pig shakes her head, her face still happy but frowning more deeply. It's you, says Anna. It's not me, says Pig. It's you walking to the bus stop to catch a number forty-nine, says Anna. Forty-nine to the end of the line! yelps Anna in mock cockney. Aaargh! screeches Pig. Crap! Vile calumny! Ditto, mutters Anna, in a hoarse voice. They both hoot and screech until Pig says Shhhh! It's past eleven o'clock!

Anna stubs out the invisible butt with a verbal hiss in the saucer of her teacup, and stretches out on her bed. They look at each other, smiling. From the street they hear heavy metal shutters being pulled down across the restaurant door, and the neon light flickers off. There is still just enough street light for Pig to see as she delves into her duffel bag. She pulls out a box of salted crackers. Want one? she asks. Not right now, says Anna.

Oh, says Pig. What? says Anna. Pig rifles through her duffel bag and pulls out a small white box. In several languages it conveys the message that it has the power to turn off your running bowels like a tap. For you, says Pig. Excellent, says Anna, just what I wanted – but I didn't get you anything. Never mind, Pig counters, it's the thought that counts. She raises her biscuit in a toasting gesture. Happy Christmas, Anna, says Pig. Happy Christmas, Pig, says Anna.

THE GAP

It's a very small yellow sofa, a two-seater really, but somehow there's an enormous space between them. A Grand Canyon of dry rock and spiky plants and dust – a difficult landscape, twenty years of friendship based on unresolved attraction. A Big Sofa. In Olivia's mind at least, the Grand Canyon is also the exact size of Mary Ann.

Claiming her ground, she curls her legs up and rests her head on the elbow propped against the sofa-back. Joseph sits at an angle, legs crossed. He hasn't yet removed his jacket, and their body language is still tentative. Olivia senses that Joseph would like to touch her, more than just the ritual hug, but he only puts out his hand casually in her direction – there it is, five inches from her elbow. She would like to bridge the gap, touch this beautiful hand, brown and tapered. He wears a silver ring on the fourth finger, but Olivia suspects it has something to do with his sister's jewellery-making business, rather than his marriage.

They look at each other, talk, laugh, look away. They are flirting, aren't they? She finds it hard to read his mood. At times his eyes are opaque, his smile rare. There is tension and anger and sorrow in his face, the embodiment of a stormy sky, something she thinks she understands, which affords her a modest pride and a noble glow for a few delicious moments. Olivia tries to remember what Joseph looked like four years previously, whether his eyes had crinkled less or more on the occasion of their last meeting. Same house, same sofa. During that encounter the size of the gap was less evident to her, being filled with the invisible bulk of her recent ex-lover, cushioned by her own timidity.

Deflecting her enquiries, as he always does, Joseph asks, disingenuously, if she is 'dating'. It never seems untruthful to reply No, I'm happy being single and celibate, and it would take something compelling to change it now. But sitting there on the far side of the Grand Canyon, Joseph might be asking considerably more than that. He always asks. Olivia supposes that to mean he wants to know. She assumes he wants to know because, despite living on another continent on the other side of the Atlantic, despite his being married now, whether that was a Green Card arrangement or not, despite her own previous relationships with people he has known too, despite or because of the truths they have exchanged in their sporadic twenty-year friendship, despite the Grand Fucking Canyon, they love each other. It's on paper, sent via US mail, they love each other. So that makes her a liar, because part of her hurts every time she looks at him and talks brightly of being content in her solitude. If she thinks he's hurting too, at her blithe protestations, perhaps it will make her feel better, though not as good as she'd like. Not as good as being held and touched would feel after years of continence. Hers, not his – she is very aware of that Mary Ann-shaped fact.

So what? Nothing is going to happen between them today. Maybe never. For three days before his visit, Olivia rehearsed the arguments about why sleeping with Joseph would be out of the question. She anticipated a discussion of the topic, looked forward nervously to a chance to articulate some of her doubts and qualms. She had over fifty reasons against it, fifty where forty-nine might have been enough. Perhaps by expressing her thoughts while looking him in the eye she might believe them herself. It seemed desperate to have so many reasons crowding her mind, as though she expected him to apply pressure, to seduce her, so that she would need to use them. No, she knew him, he wasn't like that. In addition, she cursed herself for the appalling folly, the vanity, of having the idea that he might want to sleep with her at all. And for the euphemism, as though sleep had anything to do with it.

As far as she knew he was still having a sexual relationship with Mary Ann. That was not something to be tossed aside. Besides, they knew each other too well for it to be possible that one encounter would suffice, and if it were embarrassing, how could friendship be restored intact? Sex would be something close to an incestuous act, she told herself, cleaning the house, washing her hair, applying body lotion, looking for her bra. Humming, grinning at the mirror as she imagined opening the door, how he would look, what they would say on greeting, on parting. Stupid to anticipate, unthinkable to do anything but.

On the other hand, there is the mystery of the toothbrush. Poking out of his bag when he opens it to give her a sales talk on his Powerbook and the necessity of e-mail as a way they might keep in touch. What does the toothbrush mean? Is it new? Is it a veiled request, a boy-scout habit, or merely the obligatory trans-Atlantic hand-luggage for achieving dental hygiene on a quick visit with friends? She doesn't know. Maybe she doesn't really know him at all.

They go out to find a drink and dinner and the mood changes. Walking the wet pavement in greater proximity, but able to avoid each other's eyes while bumping elbows, teasing moves up a step. By the time they are settled in a noisy bar with Guinness and wine in front of them they confidently mirror each other's posture, sitting knee to knee, just a few inches away from textbook positions for Tantric intimacy. He is intuitive, responsive. Does he know what she's thinking? Is she misreading the situation, his friendliness? It has happened before.

Olivia feels a recklessness pulse through her, the three days of cautious rationalising evaporate, leaving her body on alert. She has missed this so much, the physical and intellectual pleasures of tuning in, of vibrating at the most interesting frequencies. Is it actually about Joseph, or just the absence in her life of anyone stimulating, passionate, intelligent? That's a good enough reason for most people, most of the time, but time is the operative word, and time is not in their favour. So. They talk more about relationships, psychology, pharmacology, politics.

One hundred paces to the Pizza Express. The place is quiet, the service fast and unobtrusive. Finally Joseph talks about Joseph. He will finish his doctorate, he will continue to live in America, he doesn't know what will happen with Mary Ann. The gaps around what he says are intriguing. As he articulates his concerns his face becomes less guarded, his eyes lose some of the opacity. Olivia sandwiches her slices of pizza to keep the anchovy from slithering off the cheese, and nibbles, and holds his gaze. She imagines her interest blazing from her face so strongly it washes him in light, warming and reassuring Joseph, she hopes, just as strongly as he had warmed her in his last letter.

'You know that I love you and care about you . . .' Written down as part of a longer sentence, that's easy. Up-close in a pizza restaurant half an hour from train-time, while the shadows of their personal histories colour the evening, 'I Love You' is impossible to say. Probably shouldn't be said, ever, between two people so alike, so scarred by love's sophistry. Safer to keep things light. Nevertheless she wants to say it, hear it said.

Time is running faster now. They stride towards the station. Olivia wonders what would happen if she took his arm, kissed him, made him miss the train, all this subterranean planning with no break in her stride or her cheerful conversation. Down the steps to the platform, sixty eight seconds ticking away on the enormous clock. What should they say? Gosh, it was so great to see you. Olivia comments on the steam issuing from their mouths as they exchange keeping-in-touch assurances, awkward again. A last hug. 'I wish I had more time,' Joseph says, a wave, and he steps into the carriage.

Olivia is unprepared for the sensation that engulfs her as she pads home to her beautiful, empty flat. The cocaine rush of Joseph's company keeps her awake till the small hours, when she dreams about talking to him and wrestles with the bedcovers. At 6am she seeks distraction with a novel, then an urgent work project, none of which hold her attention for a minute. She bathes, dresses, wanders from room to room, repeating the countless arguments still boiling in her head about the folly of relationships, the inevitability of co-dependence, the death of sanity, the bitter sadness of endings.

The vacuum left by Joseph's absence settles around her, spoiling the taste of cake and tea, the pleasure of afternoon sunlight hot through the window. She resents the presence of the sanctimonious telephone and the long, silent hours until she can shake off the symptoms of withdrawal.

Should she call him? She calls his father's house, leaves an innocuous message, hangs up feeling wrong-footed. Later that night she sits, bleary-eyed and blowing her nose, on the yellow sofa, communing with Joseph's lingering presence.

– I had so much fun with you. You have ruined me for other people, for nights in with the t.v., for modern novels with sassy heroines. I miss you.

Now she hopes he won't call in case she betrays herself. Obsessive introspection is not a facet Olivia likes to reveal to her friends, knowing too well that the moment you expose your vulnerabilities is the moment uneasiness and contempt gain a foothold. She reflects on how dismissively they'd joked, she and Joseph, a few hours ago, about 'The Rules', the social fauxpas of revealing your emotions. How easy it is to laugh at theoretical wounds, when you haven't yet felt the knife, slipping up under your own ribs to twist in the gap below your heart.

BLUEBEARD

Early on the morning of her third wedding anniversary, Jane got up quietly, wrapped herself in a kimono, and went to the airing cupboard. From its hiding place behind a bundle of sheets she took out her work and regarded it with some pride. It was the first piece of personal artwork she had made since she'd abandoned her post-grad year to marry Robert. The painting was acrylic on board, small but detailed, depicting a human iceberg: the head and feet out of frame, a woman's torso, ghostly white, floated in a blue Hokusai sea, nipples and belly visible above water, whilst below, her bulk descended into ink-black depths. At the edge of the picture, just beneath the surface of the water, a tiny flesh-coloured submarine aimed its periscope at the curve of a breast, and an invisible captain remarked in bubble speech 'A few small floes.'

Jane wondered if he would get it. She was tempted to scribble an explanation on the back, as she taped it into the frame, but restrained herself. She wrapped the picture in lilac tissue paper, tied it with a silver ribbon, and took it with a cup of coffee into the bedroom.

– Happy anniversary she said, rumpling his hair. Robert woke with a lot of gummy yawning and groaning. She left him to it, made herself tea and toast, and came back. He had pulled himself up on one elbow and was making faces at the coffee.

– Open it, then.

– What is it? He tore the wrapping off carelessly, reached for his spectacles, studied it with his mouth open, murmuring indistinct and non-committal sounds of discovery. When he met her eyes it was clear he was puzzled.

– It's great. Wow. Darling. Did you do this?

– Mmhm. Do you like it?

– Of course, darling, thank you.

He pursed his lips and blew her a kiss. No, he didn't get it. Maybe a few weeks of it hanging on the wall and it would start to register. For the rest of the day she struggled to suppress the impulse to say, Well, how about me? Bunch of roses? Box of roses? Wee token of esteem? Hmm? and failed. Robert's consequent embarrassment made her feel guilty. She heard the voice of a hundred spinsters inside her head telling her that being taken for granted was a form of flattery and she told the voice to shut up, and then made determinedly cheerful conversation all evening to paper over the cracks in her confidence.

When their marriage was three years and seven weeks old, she took a different tack. One night she baked him chocolate brownies containing dried psilocybin mushrooms, prepared the bedroom with scented candles and hypnotic music, and emerged from the bathroom in a whispering wreath of layered silk scarves. She held her arms above her head, and swayed in front of Robert, hoping that the glimpse of her breasts through chiffon would drown his efforts at speech and analysis. As she stretched him across the bed and kissed every inch of his body, he described the experience objectively in lavish, fractal, pixilated detail and then fell asleep inside her. In the morning, he patted the top of her head on his way to the front door and said he'd try to be home for supper. He wasn't.

She sought advice. Her best friend said leave him. Her sister said he was a fool. Her mother suggested counselling and a crash diet. Her intelligence reminded her that she was herself to blame for having expectations. She didn't want to give up on him, she wanted to renew his interest, to rekindle the flame, to snare his curiosity. She wanted him to get out of the submarine and explore the rest of her land mass. The Terra Firma of her intellect, her bi-polar energies.

Robert was wooed every day for a week – poems under his pillow, lilies sent to his office, salmon-en-croûte in his lunch bag; she had her hair cut and tinted, wore her most revealing clothes, retiled the bathroom. She cooked Thai, Indian, French provincial and comfort foods. She made no overt demands until the Friday night when she lay in wait for him in an inviting posture across the sofa, but when he entered the room it was with the fixed intention of watching American Football and he merely asked her to shift over. She retreated to the kitchen and made him popcorn with butter and cajun seasoning, brought him a beer, smiled. Then she went to bed with a good book, which was not enough to keep despair from creeping into her mind.

That night she dreamed of the Tuareg. Draped in white samite, mystic, wonderful, a *Clothes Show* make-over but still sporting that traditional blue, she rode a camel through a sea of sand, headcloth fluttering in the breeze, a flag of bondage. She lay in a tent with Rudolph Valentino smouldering beside her on the heaped carpets, his kohl-lined eyes searching deeply into her soul. Beneath her robes she trembled and sweated, her skin pale and stained where the blue dye of the nomads veined her like marble. As Rudolph reached out for her, she stepped aside from the dream and looked at herself for for a while, noting the effect, as a painter does, of white and blue and shadow and light. And in the morning when she woke she had a new idea.

When Robert returned from work the following evening he found a note pinned to the front door: ENTER WITHOUT RESERVATION. DO NOT BE ALARMED, IT IS ONLY ART. Robert was alarmed. Because he was an architect, he knew little of art, not even what he liked. Art frightened him, with its curvy lines and bold colours, threatened him with its obscure, sly hints at things he had not experienced.

The flat was dark and warm, all the doors closed and the hall light switch failed to fulfil its function. Robert put down his coat and briefcase and listened to the silence. Noticing the faint glow from under the living-room door, he opened it with caution. The curtains were drawn, the furniture moved back against the walls. Centre stage, three anglepoise lamps fitted with daylight-simulation bulbs focused cool beams down on to the dining table where atop a dark-blue sheet there stretched a nude. She lay like carving on a tomb, sepulchral, skin luminous, eyes closed. Robert was unused to the sight of Jane inanimate, and while a part of his mind complained at the theatricality of the situation another part pricked into life, recognising an admiration for her ingenuity and humour, an exhumation of dormant sentiments. He stepped up to the tableau nervously, as if afraid to waken Sleeping Beauty. She appeared to be wearing some sort of lower garment, bikini sized, textured, woven? Was it a trick of the light? He drew closer, drew and held a breath.

Beside the powdered ivory skin, the astonishing electric blue of her pubic hair rose in whirls and spirals like vegetation from a sci-fi film set. He thought of coral, roses, heather, fur, feathers, tweed, all blue, as though something had slid between his eyes and his brain and tinted the world uniquely. Closing his eyes he sensed her presence. In his imagination, his tongue explored her textures, the peaks of meringues, the crunch, the slight resistance and melting softness below; felt the soft scrape of an old toothbrush; the tingle of sherbet. He leaned close, and filled his nostrils with the scent of talc and beneath it something apricot and peppery. She didn't smell blue, and the contrast delighted his senses even further.

– Jane – Jane. . . . Wait, I'll be right back!

Very, very slowly, the sculpture started to smile.

Jane remained silent whilst Robert took photographs of her from every conceivable angle.

That night, as they lay close and comfortable, Jane thought she'd achieved success. Robert looked into her eyes, the same eyes he'd proposed to only years before, kissed her on those same lips and asked, with a tentative return to his once playful manner, if she might repeat the operation, soon, with a change of colour. She went one better, arranging the use of a friend's house where the pink walls would clash with the yellow colourant she had in mind. The week after that, she hung aluminium foil in the spare room and used bronze paint. In the following weeks she used every colour she could find, and added further elements, making her body a salad, an oasis, a seascape, an animal. She dredged the local charity shops for odd mirrors and pieces of fabric to use as props. Robert began to come home early from work, stayed up later at night, reading art theory. In the evenings when they were not photographing, he took a course in colour printing, and began to compile a portfolio.

By their fourth anniversary, Robert's photographs had been exhibited in London, featured in two Sunday glossies, discussed on *Review*, and rushed into publication. He was hailed as the brilliant successor of Helmut Newton, Archimboldo, Vincent Van Gogh, and Jeff Koons. He was championed and savaged by critics of all sexes, declared the darling of the talk-shows, and much collected, principally by the Japanese. When inevitably the invitation came to show in New York, it was hand in hand with a *South Bank Show* request to document the event on film. Jane was pleased for him. She appeared in the background in some of the magazine photos, a mysterious, bland figure, out of focus, bearing no resemblance to the exotic creature in his work. Robert referred to her only as Jane, as though she were a fictional person.

Preparing for the New York show, Robert was preoccupied, difficult, distant, sexless. He spent time with agents and publicity people, and had no time for anything but the work. *His* Work. Months had passed since their last photo session, but Jane consoled herself with the thought that New York would provide them both with inspiration. She began a diary to record in detail the colours that corresponded to her nightly dreams, and tried to discuss them with Robert. But, as his career took off, their relationship changed again. He seemed to Jane to have become someone she no longer recognised. Physical characteristics she thought she'd taken for granted surprised her anew – the shape of his nails, the smell of his clothes, his night-time rituals in the bathroom all seemed strange to her. When she had overcome her initial shock at the realisation, it gave her another one to think that she had sunk her hopes in this man's abilities to care for her. She could feel her wounds closing, as she pushed him out of the forefront of her consciousness, though they still smarted when she realised he had been doing it for so much longer and was cured of love. The course of her recuperation was more protracted and more painful.

Robert's US agent had arranged for a two-month lease on a TriBeCa loft with a view of the river. The space was massive: four separate sleeping platforms, luxurious bathrooms with sunken tubs, a prosciutto-coloured marble kitchen that defied spillage or waste – the whole place a vulgar, chrome-plated parody of the traditional artist's garret. In return for this opulence Robert was on view twenty-four hours a day, surrounded by sycophants, sucker fish along for the ride on a potential Big Fish. Jane was soon excluded from most of the preparation activities, which seemed largely to consist of eating, smoking and bitching at prominent tables in expensive restaurants. Robert was deified, robed, honoured, offered exclusive memberships, recreational substances, invited everywhere. Vacuous-looking people in extraordinary clothing drifted around the apartment at odd hours, their function unclear, their attitude to Jane cool verging towards hostile. Robert slept alone and ate out, pleading convenience, and to save face Jane took to escaping in the afternoons for a couple of hours of walking, soon stretching the hours into days and nights. The city seeped into her consciousness more and more, so that she felt at home, able to belong to it and it to her. Extending her chameleon nature, she made café acquaintances, people who reminded her of her early ambitions and parts of herself that had found no expression with Robert were brought back into focus. She filled notebooks with ideas and sketches, and made a series of regular appointments at a seedy establishment in the Village to discuss her 'concepts'.

Passing Robert in the hallway of the apartment one

morning, Jane realised that she no longer felt inclined to ask him how he was, or what was happening with his work. She stopped and looked at him. He met her gaze, blankly. A stranger. White noise filled her head, she looked away, and they passed on without exchanging a syllable. Jane took this as a tacit agreement that their lives as partners had terminated, and enjoyed an immediate surge of confidence in the plans that she had been quietly formulating. Meanwhile, Robert was receiving horizontal inspiration. Ursula was a model, emaciated, 6 ft 2, taciturn and, most importantly, albino. She had no visible body hair, and shaved her head – a perfect canvas. Secretly, Robert planned a new book, in shades of white.

When the moment of the opening arrived, the New York show was huge. A crowd gathered in front of the gallery, where a dozen security guards were deployed to heighten the tension and underline the importance of the event. Limousines circled the block, depositing thousands of kilos of designer-clothed flesh on to the sidewalk to be eyed and envied. Already inside the building, Robert was giving telephone interviews and fretting over the whereabouts of his wife. His agent assured him his office had issued her an embossed, gold-edged invitation to join them for a launch-lunch, but she had not shown, nor had she contacted the gallery or indeed left any message at all, not so much as a good luck token. Suddenly her absence irked Robert. Things would seem less than perfect without her passive approval, her nominal presence. Come to think of it, he couldn't recall when they had last spoken in person.

But forget Jane, it was his day. Champagne corks popped discreetly but on time, regardless of her absence. Robert warmed to the enthusiasm of the guests, flattered by the flutters of applause, the open admiration. He walked like a minor God through the room, arms reaching out to greet and touch. Hands were pressed, cheeks kissed, personal cards were slid into his pockets, and the little red labels came out in a rash as dollars were spent by plastic. Gliding three steps behind Robert, in a floor-length white-velvet coat, Ursula smiled enigmatically enough to encourage the rumours already circulating, but when questioned merely allowed her gaze to rest on the back of Robert's head, one taloned finger to her colourless lips, anaemically Shirley Temple cute.

On a dais in the centre of the gallery, a microphone waited patiently for Robert. His agent gave an Oscar-worthy introduction, the crowds parted, murmuring and rustling catalogues, as Robert stepped on to the platform. He looked at the faces looking back at him. So many eyebrows, so many mouths, noses, an ocean of features repeating in waves as far as the back of the room. Only Ursula, featureless, stood out, her head a full pallid moon reflecting his own glowing fame.

And as his pride swelled into speech he opened his mouth to say a few humble words, he opened his mouth and drew breath, and held it. A second luminous figure appeared in his view, walked towards him, small and slight, clothed in white samite, mystic, wonderful, but still sporting the traditional indigo headcloth. The blue of her eyes was all there was of Jane, and he was surprised that he recognised them, surprised that they were blue, unconscious that he had gazed into these eyes once with such passion that he could have painted them, if only he'd felt the inclination, if only he'd possessed any artistic ability. As the assembly grew silent and formed a circle encompassing the new arrival, she stopped.

Slowly the turban unravelled and folded to the floor. Her skull was shorn, her eyes brilliant, kohl-lined, her lips crimson. The white robe shimmered as it slid inch by inch from her shoulders, her arms, her hips, and pooled at her feet.

The markings started at her neck. The angry red had faded, the scars healed, and now her tattoos stood proudly, fresh and blue-black on her creamy skin. The lines were fluid, curving, singing, relating all parts of her body to the viewers. In the language of symbols they spoke of her life, and the life of every other woman in the room. They told the story of the purpose of love and the meaning of pain, of emptiness and fulfilment, of passions lost and found, creation and death. When she raised her arms a ripple of emotion ran through the crowd and women began to weep, strangers turning to each other to seek recognition of their common condition. When she turned to reveal the rythmns on her back, men blanched and covered their mouths in gestures akin to shame. With her eyes closed, Jane stepped free of her garments and began to dance.

Long Shot

4 May 1999: 12.45pm

She looked through her notes one last time in the taxi. Questions, list of references to his early work, Press Association background, Internet Database gossip, quotes from fellow actors, male and, more to the point, female. Satisfied that she had done as much preparation as there had been archive material to uncover, she folded the A4 sheaf into her bag, and withdrew a mirrored compact. Her complexion was still porcelain, lipstick intact, every hair silken, strands of gold and bronze subtle against her own deeper brown. Okay, you can stop fussing now, she told herself, the new look works. Finally she checked the tape recorder, cassettes, back-up batteries, credit cards and cash, then leaned back into the cushioned vinyl and closed her eyes. Obsessive. Compulsive. Obsessive-compulsive. The words fitted themselves to the throb of the taxi's diesel engine, halted at traffic lights, until red turned to amber and the gears changed rhythm.

Arriving ten minutes early, she was genuinely surprised and slightly annoyed to see him already seated. The restaurant had been his choice, an establishment familiar with celebrity and discretion. Light flooded in jewel colours from the 1930s original stained glass across the damask-dressed tables, sug-gesting different ambiences for dining, business or pleasure; his table was washed with pink and blue, and his shirt was a soft lilac rendered oddly student-bohemian by the patterned glow. Beside his plate was a copy of *Birthday Letters*, three pages earmarked. He took off a pair of titanium-framed spectacles as she crossed the room to his corner.

– Teresa Gordon? Hi, Nial Reeves.

They shook hands, the one-professional-to-another, firm-clasp-for-four-beats-and-release experience she had been expecting. She sat, he sat. He scrutinised her for a moment, with a slight wariness.

– Have we met before?

– Oh, I've got one of those faces – or maybe it's the Jennifer Aniston hair.

– It suits you.

He offered her a Gitane, didn't ask for consent before lighting up, caught the eye of the waiter and asked for mineral water, a bottle of Sancerre, and the menu in ten minutes. And now we have established who's in control, thought Teresa, let the game commence.

They made small talk about publicity and media gossip, while she arranged the Sony next to a vase of freesias, tried to stop her hands shaking, and maintained eye contact as she pressed record/play. Close-to, his face was nothing special, the eyes small and narrow, the chin sharp, the mouth ordinary. His hair was already thinning, and the skin beneath his eyes was puffy. Still, the man was attractive. Money and success had added to his natural confidence, and hours at the gym ensured that muscles rippled where they should, even under a linen shirt. Whatever else his recent Hollywood experiences had taught him, his smoking technique was now a long way from the back of the bike sheds. You could take the boy out of Paisley . . .

– D'you mind if we do the born-and-brought-up bit, Nial?

– Sure, okay; 1964, near Glasgow, got four GCSE's, first job as an apprentice electrician, blah blah. You know all this stuff, everybody's heard it before . . .

– And they always want to hear it again. But what made you apply to Drama School? That must have been a big leap in the dark for you?

– Yeah, well, it was and it wasn't. I don't think about it.

Sensitive area, Teresa noted. His voice, which one columnist had likened to Brando on porridge oats, took on a nasal tone when things weren't going entirely his way, not a quality he used in his work – it made him sound tougher, less attractive, and conversely vulnerable. They ambled through the first course, a terrine of wild mushrooms, Teresa prodding him about early t.v. experiences, his move into film, the money, the stars he had worked with. She eased up during the grilled halibut to let him enthuse about his next project, the reason he had agreed to do this interview, a return to the London stage in a specially written comedy about footballers in which he would portray 'a George Best character with a lot of integrity, you know?' With most of the Sancerre inside him, and on a topic he clearly loved, his face took on some of the beauty the camera could find in it, his smile infectious, his eyes open and expressive. He ran his hands through his hair in a trademark gesture said to arouse passion in women everywhere. He toyed with the cutlery, as he mentioned his love for his parents, and the luck to which he owed his success. He offered her a piece of the white-chocolate cheesecake he was spooning up with a lingering sensuality, and she felt a tingle as he touched her arm to indicate the blinking battery light on her tape machine. She smiled a lot and blushed a little, gazed into his eyes, and generally behaved like a woman who couldn't believe she was being paid to spend time with screen-idol Nial Reeves: modest, sincere, handsome, manna for the hormones. Cointreau arrived with the coffee, and Teresa returned to the agenda.

– I won't ask you about all the fantastically famous women you've quote slept with unquote. I know that's off limits, but tell me about your first screen sex. How was it? Who was it?

– Teresa! I really can't remember . . .

– Oh go on – you must!

She scrabbled through her notes, found his c.v. and ran her finger down the list of credits. 'Look *Telling Porkies*, 1989, you co-starred with Emma Thompson – nope, I remember that one, didn't get your kit off – *The Maven*, filmed in Prague, 1991, you had a scene with Isabelle Huppert, just after she'd made a dire movie with Hugh Grant, that was a love story, wasn't it?

– Nope, not for me, I never got below the neck with her, it was a 12 certificate. You have a great memory, or great research skills.

– Ah, well . . . I have to confess I've had my eye on you . . .

– That's very flattering.

– No, really, I have. I've always . . . watched your career, as they say, with great interest.

A silence, while Nial, smiling, lit another Gitane and

poured more wine, underlined Teresa's admission. On Nial's part the silence indicated a comfortable acceptance of admiration, on hers, a nervousness at having offered it so blatantly. The ego-fed glint in his eye was unmistakable. She looked away and shuffled the paperwork.

– Oh! I know – that BBC drama you did, the crime thing . . .

– Uh huh. *Silent City*, where I was the photographer?

– That's it – 87, it says here. You had a different girlfriend every week just about, and half of them died horribly – wasn't there a steamy scene in the pilot? I have this memory of you – your character – chatting up a woman in a bar and the next scene she's in bed with you . . . ?

– You're right, actually, I'd forgotten that pilot. The rest of the series toned down the sex a bit, because it aired right up against the watershed, and for the States, they don't like it too explicit . . . yeah, God, that was way back.

– What was it like, doing that for the first time, practically your first t.v. role, as well?

– That's right, straight out of college . . .

– How did you rehearse the sex for filming?

– You're a real terrier, you know that? I really don't remember, Teresa . . . that probably sounds dumb but there you are, it's just work, it's so artificial. It doesn't stay in your mind, you just do it and go on to the next thing, the next project, you know? I mean it must be like that for you, people you interview?

– Hm. Sometimes. Some people are forgettable, even the so-called personalities. But then you meet others who really make an impact – besides, I have the memory of an elephant.

– And you're so unlike one in every other way . . . he offered with a grin.

– You've obviously never seen an elephant conducting an interview with John Malkovich . . .

– Really? You interviewed him?

Genuine interest.

– Couple of years ago. Only memorable because I was terrified of him, and he was such a . . .

– Cold, patronising bastard and fantastic actor? That's off the record by the way.

– Right. But thank you for putting it so succinctly!

– You're very welcome. I have worked with the guy . . .

– Of course, yes . . . actually . . . no, I shouldn't tell you . . .

– What? Go on . . . tit for tat . . .

His voice had dropped its professional sheen for the second time in the conversation. Teresa reached out to the cassette and turned it off. Nial leaned across the freesias and put a couple of fingers on the back of her hand. She looked up at him. His face said 'Trust Me', just as it did in every close-up. She wondered how far she should go.

– Well, he propositioned me.

– Really? And . . . I mean . . . ?

– I was flattered. Until – it got awkward afterwards, he was quite – off-hand. Like he'd made a mistake, but it was *my* fault . . . I don't know, maybe he didn't trust me to keep my word.

She could see him scanning the possibilities, picturing the scene from every angle, aroused by it. She hovered between portraying herself as victim or consenting adult.

– You know, something extra-curricular like that, you stop being a journalist when you turn off the tape and take off your skirt . . .

She was half-laughing, to show him it was alright to discuss it. Something not to tell the grandchildren . . . when and if . . .

– Mr Malkovich, well, well . . . Does that sort of thing happen a lot, Teresa?

– Probably not as often as it does to you, Nial.

– Touché.

He poured the last of the wine, sharing it between them, and made a toasting gesture, then downed his half-glass in two swallows. Teresa played with her glass, swirling the pale liquid, watching him. Her eyes were drawn to the movement in his throat, the way the skin stretched, moved as he drank, as he spoke.

– These situations come along, you look at them, you ask yourself 'can anyone get hurt?' and you make a choice, don't you?

He reached for the cigarettes, lit up, narrowed his eyes and blew out a plume of smoke. Very urban Clint Eastwood. Teresa leaned forward and said softly:

– And how do you know when the situation comes along?

– Teresa. You just know. Don't you?

They were exchanging longer looks then, employing that serious, lazy tone that has an edge of bluff to it, Glenn Close and Michael Douglas in an empty restaurant on a rainy afternoon, George Clooney and Jennifer Lopez in *Out Of Sight*. You just know. When the moment happened nothing was spoken, a decision reached in the tiny electrical impulses that buzzed across the table. Teresa put the Sony away in her bag, placed her credit card on her side plate, and excused herself for two minutes. When she re-emerged from the Ladies, he was waiting at the door. He took her arm as he hailed a cab.

The flat was cool but stuffy, uncomfortable in a way that interior designers call style and human beings call lack of personality. Teresa noted these things habitually, and mentally ticked the box marked 'Executive Rental'. Nial took her coat, pushed open doors to a bathroom and bedroom, and went into the shiny stainless-steel fitted kitchen, where he selected a bottle from the fridge and started looking for glasses in a series of cupboards. Teresa felt suddenly amused, as though she had fallen into a seventies script, where she was supposed to wrap herself in a fur rug and stretch across the hearth in an inviting posture, waiting for the hero to ravish her. To combat imminent hysteria, she opted for the bedroom balcony and a view of the Thames. Carrying champagne flutes, Nial joined her moments later. After only a few sips of wine their mouths became occupied with each other and they moved inside to the bed.

He peeled off his shirt and started on hers, but she slowed him, took off her shirt, skirt and bra. She prayed he wouldn't say anything obvious like 'God, you're beautiful', or 'I want you', lines she had heard him whisper with urgency in at least one TV drama, and with her breasts in his mouth she assisted the prayer quite successfully. He lay half on top of her, his right hand busy pulling at her pants, until she used her legs to flip him on to his back. She straddled him, and started unbuckling his soft leather belt, unbuttoning the fly of his 501s. He smiled up at her, but she avoided his eyes, frowning. She tugged at his jeans, and he eased them off his hips, lifting her with the movement, until he lay there in his black Calvin's. She could feel his erection through the cotton. His whole body was toned, lightly tanned, and his chest was smooth. She reached out and placed her hand across his eyes, closing them, kept it there long enough for him to get the message.

– I like what you're doing, he said. Is it okay?

– Ssh. Just follow me?

He nodded, eyes still shut. Teresa took her hand away from his face, and began to tease his chest with her nails. She closed her own eyes and rocked.

13 November 1987: 10.20am

The room was cold, and dusty, and her body felt odd, covered in goosebumps, draped in the folds of a dressing

gown that was not her own. She got into the big brass bed,
slid under the sheets, carefully, trying to avoid crumpling
the silk bedspread, wriggling out of the clumsy terry-towel-
ling robe, letting it drop to the floor. He came in, dropped
his dressing gown on the chair, his back to her, then climbed
in at the other side, still wearing red y-fronts. What she
could see of his body was white and skinny. They lay on
their backs, their heads turning towards each other to
exchange a nervous glance, then quickly away. The lights
were bright above them, and she noticed for the first time
how shabby the furnishings were, tattered red brocade on
the screen and armchair, the faux-wood panelling along the
walls, the cheap gilt-framed Degas copy above the Victorian
dressing table. On the end of the bed, her pristine, white
lacy pants, bra and suspender belt were draped, and the
sight of them prompted a nauseating surge of panic at what
she had done to get herself into this situation.

The First Assistant came to stand by the bed and looked
down at them.

– Comfy? Anything you need?

– Well, if you could all just go out for twenty minutes and
shut the door . . .

She was surprised by the confidence in her voice, the
remark itself, and the spontaneous laughter it caused
among the crew, breaking the nervous tension on the set.
The First smiled, picked up the discarded robes, and walked
over to the door. He called out:

– Clear the set – quiet, please – this is a rehearsal! In the
shadows outside the bedroom the Director talked to the
Director of Photography, standing over a black and white
monitor. The DP waved his hands at the lighting rig, then
made slow, whirly gestures; the Director nodded, adjusting
his baseball cap, pulling on his mittens. Linda, the make-up
designer, stomped past them with her array of combs and
sprays to take a last professional look at Tessa's fake tan,

Nial's fake stubble. She prodded Kirby grips further into Tessa's elaborately arranged cascade of hair, and left without saying a word. The director, Callum, came into the bedroom, and looked down at them with a paternal fondness, Daddy woodcutter saying goodnight to Hansel and Gretel before their big day in the woods.

– Okay? Good, right, we'll just rehearse this. Now, the real question is – who wants to go on top? Tessa? Good, okay . . . I'd like it a bit remote, something she's *doing* to him, 'cause he's the wee virgin here, isn't he? Take your time, though . . . and watch the sheets round the bum, okay? Are we ready, Stefan? Make it a good one, guys, we don't want to do this too often . . .

As Callum walked off to his seat by the monitor, Tessa inched her hand under the bedclothes until she felt the heat of Nial's body. She touched him, looking for his hand, but got a hairy bit of leg, cold and trembling.

– Sorry, she whispered. He grimaced.

They had met briefly, in the first instance clothed, seated next to each other in a chilly canteen while Callum chatted about the film, exchanging no more than a few desultory remarks. Then today, for a line-run, in a corner of the set, just twenty minutes before their scene together. Tessa had fluffed her third response, Nial had given her a look of scorn, and muttered 'that's not the line', cut her off, returned to his dressing room. Tessa had spent the intervening minutes shaving her armpits with a dull Gillette and cold water, and having her bikini area touched up with thick, powdery body make-up by the sullen Linda. Lastly, Callum had taken her aside, told her how nervous Nial was, as though he imagined she was the more confident. She'd said she'd do her best.

– Quiet! The First yelled, and all talk and movement stopped.

– First positions!

Tess moved fluidly across the cold sheet, swung herself up and on top of Nial. He placed his hands on her thighs, keeping his eyes on her face. He smiled at her, but she didn't respond beyond a slight flexing of her mouth. She pulled the sheets a little higher up her hips, and straightened her back, looking down at him, her hands relaxed at her sides. The faint sound of rubber-soled shoes on the feet of the camera crew, moving stealthily about their business, faded out of her consciousness until there was only this, two bodies in a bed. Then Callum called:
– Action.

4 May 1999: 4.40pm

Nial's eyelids were pale and tender where the sun hadn't reached them. His chest rose and fell peacefully, his mouth was slack, arms relaxed and spread wide across the rumpled dove-grey sheets. From the balcony, Teresa watched him doze. The air was cool and delicious, strong enough to push the fabric of Nial's kimono against her limbs, but not enough to cause goosebumps. Far across the bend in the dirty river she could just see the recognisable roofscape of her own part of the City. Cranes glinted red and yellow nest to steeples and copper domes, and her eyes followed the capricious flight of a paper bag caught by the thermals and chased half-heartedly by a solitary seagull.

13 November 1987: 12.17pm

– Cut! Check the gate. Okay, everybody ready to go again, quickly now . . .
Callum walked in looking pleased, followed by the First.
– Okay, kids, last set-up. You're doing great, that was

nice with the hair, Tessa. We'll just roll, on this next bit, see how it goes. Tessa, you go to the window. Nial, you stay under wraps, snoozing; we'll do your nudie as a separate shot, okay? Now don't move, we want to pick up from exactly where you stopped . . .

– Callum, just a thought – nipples? Are we worried about nipples for this? The First smiled briefly at Tessa, lying exposed from the waist up, and looked back at Callum, raising his eyebrows. Callum turned back and appraised the position.

– In this context, no, shouldn't be a problem. Okay, guys? Stefan, can we go again?

Muffled response from the DP and a nod from Continuity. Callum, chewing gum vigorously, gave Tessa a fleeting smile, a wink to Nial, and left the room. The camera moved into position beyond the 'window' which Tessa was to approach. Undercover, Tessa wriggled out of her flesh-coloured bikini pants, and pushed them down the bed.

– One minute, guys, just sorting the weather . . .

Outside the 'window', the dappled effect of falling rain began playing against the glass. Tessa ran her tongue across the cross on the gold chain round her neck. Nial cleared his throat.

– Positions! And . . . Camera . . .

– Rolling . . .

– . . . Speed;

– *Silent City*, scene 51, take 1.

– . . . Action . . .

Tessa sat up, stretching her arms. She pushed her hair off her face. She swung out of the bed and walked slowly across the set to the window. She leant her arms against the sill and looked out, down, left, did a minuscule double-take and then drew in her breath rapidly. She turned to look over her shoulder at the dozing Nial, then back to the window. She kept her eyes off-focus and remembered not to blink, moistened her lips and breathed rapidly.

– Cut!

– Check the gate.

The First came in quickly and placed the dressing gown round Tessa's shoulders. She shrugged her arms into it, and tied the belt. When she turned, Callum was there, and instinctively she went towards him. He held her for a minute, wrapping her in his arms from behind, till she felt secure enough to move away.

– Gate's clear!

Callum, Stefan the DP, and Andy the First conferred briefly about whether they should break for lunch as scheduled or do another take for luck. Tessa sat in the prop chair and looked at the dirty soles of her feet. The scrum broke up with Andy's shout: 'That's lunch, everybody! Thank you, back at 1.20 prompt!' Callum walked over to Tessa and held out his hand to pull her to her feet.

– You are clear for take-off! Thanks very much, Tessa. You were great. Excellent. Dead sexy. See you at the press screening.

He pecked her cheek, squeezed her hand, went to talk to Continuity. She looked around the room one last time. Nial was by the brass bed, pulling on his costume, buckling the belt on his jeans, tucking in his shirt. Tessa touched his arm. His eyes, when they met hers, were embarrassed, searching.

– Listen, thanks. I'm really sorry . . .

– What?

– You know, when we were doing it, I got pretty, well, you know . . .'

She had no idea what he meant until he dropped his eyes to his fly and made a pointing gesture with his thumb.

– Oh . . . right. Don't mention it.

She hadn't even noticed his erection.

– Well, you were certainly convincing . . .

– So were you, she replied politely.

He gathered the last of his things and they walked into the corridor leading to the production office. The place was emptying rapidly as the crew stampeded to queue for lunch.

– Listen, I've got to go, I've got to make a phone call . . . Nial ran a hand through his hair. His relief at the ending of their screen intimacy was palpable.

– Yeah, no, off you go. I'm just going to . . . you know . . .

– I'll see you later, okay?

– Yeah . . .

– Take care . . . Nial bumped her ear with his nose as he gave her a swift hug, and headed in the direction of his dressing room. Tessa went to hers. She scrubbed at the orange-brown powder on her body with a towel, and then dressed rapidly in her own clothes.

When she emerged into daylight she was disorientated, the noise outside the studios was deafening, the sky a grey heat-haze of traffic fumes. She took a minute to remember the street she was in, and started walking towards a tube station. When she was halfway there she wondered why she hadn't stopped for a pee, or a shower, or stayed for lunch, anything to wind down before re-entering the real world. For an instant she considered turning back, then she saw a taxi, hailed it, and headed for the station and the longer journey home.

4 May 1999: 4.49pm

Teresa got dressed in the bathroom. She used Nial's tooth-brush, and washed sketchily with his face-flannel. In the bedroom Nial lay, facedown now, snoring slightly, while she checked under and around the bed. She shut the French windows gently, and eased out of the room, closing the door behind her. In the living room she wrote a note and propped it against the toaster. Then she let herself out of the flat and took the lift down to the street.

It took her nearly an hour to reach home, where she checked for phone messages, tossed her bag on to the sofa, and headed for the bath. Five minutes into her soak she heard the pad of feet in the corridor and a small dark head peered round the doorjamb. Lulu sprang up to sit at the end of the bath, swishing her tail, purring quietly, and watched Teresa's leisurely soaping until the plug was pulled and the ensuing gurgling of water down the drain got on her nerves. She complained loudly and jumped on to the toilet seat, crossing her cornflower eyes and whipping her tail in indignation. Teresa wrapped herself in a big blue towelling dressing gown and flip-flopped in her slippers into the kitchen. Grievance forgotten, Lulu nudged at Teresa's ankles while she stood by the window, gazing out across the city. The sky was beginning to darken, showing a little pink, striped with fat jet trails. Her mind inevitably returned to the interview, and she shaped a few preliminary sentences as she cleaned up her breakfast dishes and stared into the freezer, but she knew they would keep, probably improve with age. She prepared a quick meal, microwaved fisherman's pie for her, tinned tuna for Lulu. She ate standing at the counter.

4 May 1999: 5.35pm

Nial slept on until his need to urinate became a bad dream in which he had been crushed in a car accident, which was somehow erotic as well as painful. Almost sleep-walking, he staggered to the bathroom and relieved himself slowly, moaning with relief. He washed his hands, splashed his face, and with the cold water memory returned immediately. He wrapped a towel round his waist and walked through the flat to the kitchen.

The note was short. 'Dear Nial, thank you for a great interview, and for a pleasurable, off-the-record afternoon. Good luck with the play – the piece will run in the first June issue, hope you like it. T.G.'

As he crumpled the note and binned it, he flashed back to images of Teresa sitting on top of him, leaning to bite his neck, her hair falling down across his face, strong hands gripping him as she gyrated. He had let her control him, use him, surprised and excited by the way she chose to ignore the string of noncommittal endearments which most women expected. He loved the way she'd told him to 'just lie there'. He was grinning as he went back to the bedroom and gathered the strewn clothes for laundering though, to his annoyance, even after stripping the sheets and searching under the bed, he still couldn't find his black Calvin Klein shorts.

4 May 1999: 6.25pm

The tape was already wound on to the correct position. Teresa settled back on the sofa with Lulu warm on her lap to watch it again. The steadicam followed her up a set of stairs, in slow motion, accompanied by an invisible blues saxophonist. She walked backwards, leading him by his tie. They kissed on the top step and he slid off his jacket. The camera moved down her body until her skirt hit the floor, showed her stepping out of it, kicking off high-heeled sandals. The scene dissolved into another, a tracking shot now, of her gently pushing him back on to the bed. A lingering close-up of her hands at his belt, the buttons popping open one by one on his fly, and her head coming down, hair brushing his belly. Dissolve to a slow pan up, across and round the foot of the bed, her body rising and falling, back arched, his hips moving under her.

Long Shot

She advanced frame-by-frame on the final sequence: Nial Reeves' face in close up, eyes shut, rapturous. Hers in profile, lips wide, eyes cool and sharp. The focus change to the pattern of rain against the window.

One last kiss.

Fade to black.

AFTERSHAVE

Do you wear aftershave? This is the question I asked the man in the lift at Debenhams last week. It was as good a way as any to start a conversation, I thought. We were going down, and maybe it was that, the warm air rising from his body while the lift descended; he had a perfume of wood and tweed that could have come from a bottle, or it could have been just him, Derek or Oswald or whoever he was.

He looked at me out of the corner of his eye, the left eye, a brown eye, with heavy lashes, and his mouth moved as though he was going to speak. He fixed me in his partial gaze, he leaned towards me, I felt his breath on my face as he said,

– Pardon?

Had he really not heard me? Was he kidding? Only the two of us in the damn lift, and I felt silly standing next to him in total silence during the journey. I say journey because time stretches, in lifts. Like the Tardis.

We'd been standing there shoulder to shoulder, not touching, but lined up, soldiers on parade, sardines in a little tin can on wires, ever since the top floor. Had he been a woman we might have smiled and discussed why department stores make you walk half a mile between up escalators, or the appalling cost of fresh cream chocolate éclairs. But he was a man. Young and freshly shaved, and good looking if you find that interesting. I don't particularly, but I wanted to know if he had character behind the smooth chin and sleek hair. Life is precious, every moment, every encounter, could be your last – so why waste time on conversation in lifts, you're thinking?

Well, say the lift got stuck, or worse, say the cables broke and we plummeted to our deaths. I'm in that box for the rest of my life potentially, am I not? All too few breathless moments of it, maybe. And if this stranger and I were going to die tragically together in a matter of minutes, we'd better get acquainted. You don't particularly want your last conversation to be about aftershave, no, but you have to start somewhere. This was an ideal test situation, a rehearsal for the real thing, if not the real thing itself.

He kept his eye on me. I enunciated again,

– Are you wearing aftershave? His face froze, and mentally I ran through the list of possible answers. Yes. No. Pardon? Are you a nutter? Don't speak to me, you horrid little old person. Just as I began to wonder whether a fortyish woman really would seem ancient to a man of twenty five or thereabouts, he spoke.

– Job interview.

Job interview? By Chanel? Job interview, the new bargain basement scent by Lentheric? I voiced neither of these fleeting quips, just

– Ah.

– My ehm, my girlfriend insisted.

– She wanted you to make a good impression?

– Mm. She works at Debenhams. Gets all these free samples.

– Ah. How nice.

– We've just had lunch. In the canteen.

– Oh.

– It isn't actually aftershave. It's moisture balm. Comes in a wee blue tube. It doesn't sting.

– Really?

And we could have gone on like that, he becoming gradually more enthusiastic, me less, except that then the unthinkable happened. The lift stopped. The doors remained shut. Our heads swivelled to the rank of buttons. The only one that was illuminated read 'Emergency'.

Eggbert or Oswald pushed a few other floor number buttons at random, but nothing happened. I leaned over and pushed the Emergency button. It continued to glow proudly. A distant ringing sound came from outwith the lift, the sort of noise alarms make in your dreams, if you dream about lifts getting stuck, which I do. We looked at each other, and he suddenly did seem rather beautiful, despite the nasty lighting and his natural pallor. Sentimental of me to care now, perhaps, but his appeal was evident, and I was grateful for it. And of course, as our eyes locked, we saw each other's fear. It crossed my mind that it would be perhaps the only opportunity in our respective lives for me to play the tragic heroine, and he the cool sophisticate. On the other hand, I could crush him maternally to my bosom and soothe his tears, if he broke down, and we might actually enjoy my being an older woman for a few brief moments. But which role to adopt?

It doesn't do to plan too far ahead, for in fact he took another tack, one I hadn't expected. He started to kick the walls of the lift rather viciously, hysterically, I think is a suitable word, and swore with some skill that he'd kill or maim the person responsible for making him miss his job interview. This seemed to me to be missing the point.

– Excuse me, but I really think you're missing the point. He stopped kicking, but turned to me with such a glare in his eyes that he suddenly looked like a young Richard Burton, and I revised my imaginary scenarios to include angry and poetic passion.

– What point?

– Well, I mean, it could be worse than just missing a job interview, couldn't it? Say we're stuck here for hours? I haven't had lunch and I'd like to go to the bathroom. None of these may be an option we shall freely enjoy ever again. And that being the case, pounding the walls of the lift may be something of a futile, not to say dangerous, gesture. Hmm?

His eyes went blank for a while as the thought percolated, and then looked slightly abashed, his mouth taking on the curve of a pouting ten year-old who has been denied toffee. Slowly, he slid down the carpeted wall of the lift and sat on the floor, arms propped on his knees, head between his rather nicely manicured hands.

Meanwhile, the musak, which I should have mentioned had been dithering merrily in the background, stopped. Normally the absence of instrumental country 'n' western would have seemed a blessed relief, but on his occasion I feared it might herald something worse. And somehow the silence *was* worse. The alarm bell still rang, strong and distant, but there were no sounds of rushing feet, no brawny firemen calling our names and promising to have us out in a jiffy. Of course they wouldn't have known our names, but we would have introduced ourselves through an air duct or something. Then Osbert or Hugo would have to come clean, and so would I, but at least we might avoid all that silly Mizz business. Rather nice though, just to be citizens A and B, stuck in a lift. A feature film would be made about our desperate struggle for air, our last moments together, holding hands, reciting the 23rd Psalm, and the messages of love and despair and wisdom left scribbled on the mirror with my Fuchsia Joy Max Factor lipstick. Hugo or Eggbert did look a little like Keanu Reeves, and I'd always hoped to be portrayed by Holly Hunter, though I can't see it as natural Hollywood casting. Just please, PLEASE, not Demi Moore or Alec Baldwin. Quite wrong, utterly wrong.

– Keanu Reeves, I mumured.

He raised his head, and the look on his face at that moment was much more Charlie Brown than Keanu Reeves.

– You, you look a little like Keanu Reeves. Admittedly *he* would look a *smidge* out of place in a lift in Debenhams in a pink lycra wetsuit, but on the other hand he'd probably have been wriggling down cables looking for bombs in about thirty seconds flat . . .

– What are you talking about?

Goodness, he sounded annoyed. I suppose I'd dashed his ego. Perhaps he was more of a Hubert, after all, and obviously no film buff.

– What is your name? I asked with just a touch of asperity.

– Alec.

Oh Dear. Well, if he was going to be Alec . . .

– I'm Holly. Now we've been introduced, perhaps we could get down to brass tacks.

– I don't understand.

– I'm suggesting that we put our heads together and find a

way out, whether literally, or as a way of passing the time until we are either rescued or suffocated by our own noxious emissions. What do you think?

Alec – horrid name – stood up, with his mouth open in a most unattractive way, and sent his gaze travelling about the lift as though he were a basset hound watching a bumble bee, finally fixing on the floor again. He pointed, if you'll excuse the doggy metaphor, to his find – a floor panel. Wasn't there an Edgar Allan Poe story of that name? In this case, our panel was cut into brown linoleum, edged with grubby metal strips and displayed no visible means of lifting, or hinges. Alec hauled and grunted and strained and scrabbled to no avail for a few minutes, and it was not until I offered him the use of my metal nail file that we managed to prise up the panel and reveal – a very small opening. Once again Alec's face fell into a perplexed pout. Luckily, however, I myself am petite, and not easily dismayed.

I hiked up my Betty Jackson and knelt at the edge of the pit – ah, that's it, Poe and the Pit, not the Panel – as I say, I knelt and peered down into the darkness to see what I could see. If you've ever gazed into a well you'll appreciate the slightly different experience of looking down a lift shaft, because instead of a dank watery chill there is only dust and some sort of grease with which I expect the mechanism is kept in working order, or not, as the case may be. As Alec peered nervously over my shoulder I caught again the scent of his job-interview balm, mingled with sweat, not unpleasantly.

– How tall is this building? I asked him. Men always know these things.

– I don't know, he answered.

I snapped my fingers at him, and he looked puzzled.

– Coins, Alec, coins; we have to find out how far down we are.

Aftershave

He fumbled in his pocket, brought out a handful of
pound coins. I could see his thoughts flit across his brows
and lodge in the lines around his mouth.

– Do you have any, er, change?

I simply heaved a sigh, and looked at him, until, reluc-
tantly, he slid the money into my outstretched palm.

One one thousand, two one thousand, three one thousand, four one thousand, five – clink. I got up, dusting my
knees, and returned his remaining pounds to Alec, then
stepped back against the wall of the lift, and attempted
some mental arithmetic. I thought aloud.

– If it takes one pound coin four and a half seconds to
reach the floor of a lift shaft, how many . . . no; how heavy
is a pound coin, anyway? How long does it take a lift
holding two people to ascend one floor? Oh blast. Alec,
come on, I'm sure this is just the kind of thing you excelled
in at school. What was your best subject?

– History. European history, actually. I know a lot about
Napoleon's retreat from Russia.

– Well, unless Napoleon retreated in a lift, we're not
much further on, are we? What did you do with your A level
in history?

– Well, at the moment I'm working for a real estate
company.

– As? Doing?

– Er, I go around putting up 'For Sale' notices. And then I
take them down. Of course, it's not what I really want to
do . . .

– And what's that – presumably your interview was to be
a career move? I know, I know, I'm sounding a little testy, a
mite unsympathetic, Alec, I'm sorry, please ignore it, and go
on –

His face took on the glow of a Born Again Christian.

– I want to work in Advertising.

Creativity, lateral thinking, talent with words, personal

initiative – Alec appeared to have none of them. But I didn't
see how someone with his looks could fail in Advertising,
especially if he were to cut his hair extremely short and
adopt a more arrogant slouch or grow it extremely long and
wear crushed linens. The dark suit he had on was all wrong,
but strangely, the scent was right, he had a creative aroma.

– And this interview?

The maternal role I had sketched out for myself earlier
was coming in useful after all.

– Copy writer – I'm on a shortlist. I don't suppose I've got
a chance of getting there now, and they won't see me again.
He balled his fists and punched the wall. Very Keanu.

– Nonsense, Alec, here's what you do. Go in late, fasci-
nate them with your excuse, wave your arms about, em-
broider, pitch it to them like a movie script – you've seen
The Player, haven't you? I promise you, they'll be thrilled.
But don't apologise. I'm sure Saatchi and Saatchi never
apologise. All you need is a bit of charisma . . .

– That's it, I've got it, he said, smiling for the first time.
What a good-looking young man.

– That's what? I said, smiling back.

– Charisma. It's the aftershave balm I'm wearing. My
girlfriend said it would bring me good luck.

And he started to laugh. Within twenty seconds we were
both gasping, clutching our sides, and then each other, tears
rolling down our cheeks, speechless with laughter. Every
time we drew breath one of us would say 'charisma' and off
we'd go.

We laughed so hard we didn't notice the Emergency light
had gone, the alarm had stopped and the lift was moving.
Suddenly the door pinged open and the first thing that met
our eyes was not a horde of merry rescuers, not a raging fire
or a crowd of terrorised customers, but a tangle of electrical
equipment and a red sandwich-board sign which an-
nounced: Closed For Repairs.

Aftershave

A tiny man with a ragged moustache peered at us through safety goggles, wiped his hands on his overalls, and whined.

– Youse are no supposed tae be in here, this lift is closed, closed for repairs, it's out of action, can you not read?

He pointed righteously to his sign.

Alec took my arm. His fingers were warm through the silk of my blouse, and my chin came perfectly to the height of his padded shoulders. I looked up at his profile and experienced a sense of delicious and proprietorial anticipation. He gave my arm a squeeze and we stepped out of the lift. As we passed the little man, Alec held out his hand, and dropped five pound coins into the oily, wizened palm.

– Buy yourself some Charisma, he said.

Incomplete

As soon as I put down the phone, I start to shake. The clock reads 2.34am. The time isn't significant, but as I dress I make an equation: 34 multiplied by 2 equals 68, his age. A birthday has just passed, I sent him a novel by Peter Ackroyd and a half ounce of Old Holborn. Perhaps it was that, one half ounce too many.

In the taxi, a distant memory startles me from numbness. I was twelve. He listened, smiling, over supper, as I boasted nervously that now I thought I knew all my times tables. Later, rolling a cigarette in the light of the green shaded lamp on the roll-top desk, he offered me half a crown for each one I could reel off correctly. One to six are easy enough, so I started out with confidence, locking my hands behind my back like a Victorian child reciting 'The Boy Stood On The Burning Deck'. He stopped me, told me to start with nine. I stammered, I was silent, I wept with frustration and, ashamed, ran from the room. From that moment till this, I have avoided any situation in which I might be required to demonstrate numerical dexterity. But tonight the figures clicked in my head without a halfcrown in prospect.

I reach the hospital before the rest of the family. Following a numbers and arrows system, I make my way to the Intensive Care Unit. In the corridor outside, by the window looking out into the black night, people pace and smoke. The nurse, a little Irish girl, barely nineteen, kindly shows me to his bed, and I look down at him. They've got the wrong man. This small, pale figure lying amidst the tubes, clamps and post-surgical paraphernalia is not my father. He has no dignity left to him, stripped away along with his clothes and his consciousness. This man is thin and weak and vulnerable.

The place is hushed, with undercurrent murmurs. The sudden laugh of a nurse in the office down the hall, too loud, the sound of life continuing. The regular bleeps and twitters from the gadgetry keeping my father alive. The smells, chemical and human, pleasant and unpleasant, cologne from the pulse points of old ladies visiting their by-pass relatives, the fading Saturday-night aftershave from dutiful sons. Institutional tannin. The glare of neon lighting bounces off shiny eau de nil walls increasing the pallor of his skin. Hidden by yellow curtains, the people round the neighbouring bed discuss the relative merits of Quality Street and spray carnations as get-well gifts. I want to stop them all. I'd like to silence them with a snap of my fingers, send them into deep space, far beyond recovery by future space missions.

Incomplete

I pull up a plastic chair and sit at the bedside. His eyes are closed, lips without colour, hands by his sides above the sheets. I know he's alive only because the machines above and beside the bed tell me so. The skin on his arms is cool and papery to the touch, even the hairs on his forearms seem to have lost their vigour. I remember these hands using a spade, digging beds for roses and lilies, forking manure from the milkman's horse, laying a cobbled path. Writing furiously with yellow Bic pens in his diary. Patting the dog.

There comes a tide in the affairs of men, etc. Thank you, Jack Bruce. Words are no good. Words are thoughts translated into speech, evidence of love, and other emotions. What can I say to him now? I'm sorry for everything? I'm sorry you're in pain, I'm sorry you smoked for forty-three years, I'm sorry you didn't take up yoga or jogging, and I'm sorry you had a fondness for bacon and eggs. Is this what he'd want to hear from me?

I wish I'd read the books you were interested in. Teach Yourself Arabic, or Archery. You gave me paperbacks full of potential and I ignored them in favour of television. I wish you'd asked me about my own interests. You had never heard of Erté, or seen films by Cocteau as having any worth. You hated *Alias Smith and Jones*. You loathed abstract art, contemporary music, any form of youth culture. You put tomato ketchup on my first-ever quiche, drowning out the flavour of expensive tinned salmon. You never ate an apple until someone had peeled, cored and quartered it for you. You drank your tea strong, six sugars, and tepid.

Why am I using the past tense? Is this an epitaph? Am I getting ready to let you go? Were you ever really here? For all the things you've never told me, for all the questions I never asked, I'm sorry. I'm sorry, for fuck's sake!

Being angry with an unconscious father is a little crazy, but if I talk, can I get through to him, will he hear me? I lean forward, take his hand.

– Dad. It's me. It's Beth. No change on the monitors. People do this for days, weeks on end, sometimes. Is he playing possum, lying doggo, waiting to see if at last I'll commit myself to comment on our relationship? Has he been waiting all along for me to make the first moves?

Another memory. I brought him tea in bed. 'Thank you, darling, he said. Have you been using nail polish?' My stubby teenage hands relinquished the cup quickly and hid behind my back as I muttered, 'Yes – no, I don't know,' and fled from the room. Outside, I examined my nails, scraped furiously at the vestigial pearly lacquer applied furtively in Boots. Why was I always running away from you? Why didn't you follow? It's apparent to me now that we were always strangers, but not why we had to be.

Once again I examine my nails, pushing at the cuticles. The pain is almost welcome. Against the starchy sheets, his fingernails, so like my own, slightly ridged, conical, glow healthy and pink, an unlikely sign of vigour compared to what I know of his last few years, his last twelve hours. I lay my hand on top of his, and it fits, like the final piece of a jigsaw.

I close my eyes and try to think myself into his mind, into his body, an invading but friendly organism rallying the troops of his own defence corps.

Inches behind me, a cough I recognise, and a question.
– How is he?

Before I can reply, my sister continues,
– Have you been here long? We couldn't get the car started, and it's been snowing out our way, so I told Brian to go slow, better safe than sorry. One of the penalties of living out of town, I suppose. Anyway, we're here now. So, how is he?

I have to breathe deeply, swallow my first thoughts and count to ten, so before I can answer Brian arrives and gives a repeat performance, with an additional 'Hell parking the car.' They say shock takes people in different ways, but my sister and her husband appear to think this is an occasion for social niceties. I glance at Clare's handbag, half expecting her to have brought snacks. Struck by my own pettiness, I attempt solidarity in the shape of an awkward embrace, failing to disarm my own anxiety, and, I suddenly realise with guilt at the inappropriateness of such a thing, jealousy. She was always the one who talked to him, comfortably, naturally, a simple pipeline to God, approval always there when needed. She learned early that sitting on his knee was the best first move a girl could make with a man. Now, she does the next best thing, sitting opposite me, taking up his other hand, and a familiar despair pushes into my field of emotions. I want his love and approval for myself, exclusively, even when he's unconscious.

I lean forward over the bed, stroke my father's cheek, touch an eyebrow with one finger. We have rarely been so intimate. I was thirteen when he stopped hugging me. Later, I worked it out, his delicacy, his desire not to impose, his shyness. When I was thirty, and well past the angry stage, I started making a point of touching him, a rub on the shoulders, a clasp of hands in passing, a kiss on the bald patch when I went up to bed. A current buzzed between us, too strong to breach, impossible to discuss.

– Did Mum phone? She phoned you first, didn't she? Have you seen her yet? Probably gone for a cup of tea.

I haven't said a word but there are voices screaming inside my head – leave him with me, if he's going to die I want to spend five minutes alone with him, five silent minutes to say whatever needs to be said, telepathically, make my peace, receive his blessing and let go. Shove off, you and your boringly nice Brian, this is nothing to you, just a little dramatic hiccup between golf and your next dinner party. I know I'm being unfair, I know I am, but I don't want her here. My personal anxiety takes up all the available emotional energy, and Clare is a distraction with her silly handbag, and her mundane chit-chat. She doesn't need to be here, there is no unknowing for Clare, no guilt, no angst, no dark question in her placid existence. No doubt about being loved.

I am suddenly conscious of how much pain I feel, in my head and my chest, of how rigidly I am holding myself. Surprised also at the rage, a sort of boiling noise in my inner ear, like white water reaching the top of a deep fall. I lean back into the plastic chair and look around me. There is my sister, two feet away, quietly weeping tears I hadn't heard in her voice, tears I haven't seen since her wedding day. Her hair tumbles down her shoulders over the blue wool coat, and Brian has a hand on her upper arm, and an unusual look of compassion and intelligence on his face, and I'm struck by the image, the holy couple in silent prayer, like the card I had stuck in the mirror in my cubicle at boarding school as an inducement to piety, a reminder of faith. It hadn't worked for me, loneliness was stronger magic and I became an adept. I cried most nights, and now recall with a rush of nausea the texture of the tartan blanket, which smelled of home, against my face as I slept. The memory threatens my equilibrium. When I push abruptly up from the chair it voices a horrible squeal, but I leave the ward without a word to my sister or a look back.

The night is still and cool. Three figures on the bench by the bus stop sing a ballad with the sentimentality of Carlsberg Special patriotism. The business of placing one foot in front of the other and regulating my breathing allows me to alter the focus of my thoughts, encouraging a short poem to develop from the rapid gait at which I am striding the slick pavement. Left, right, left, right, live, you bastard, live, you bastard, live, you bastard, live . . .

I don't know how long it takes to get home, but I find myself automatically putting the key in the lock, entering my flat. I fill and switch on the kettle, sweep a pile of newspapers off a kitchen chair and sit. The timer on the central heating reads 3.45am. After a few moments I draw a pen towards me, and a writing block, and begin to make a list of things to do tomorrow, no, today, in a few hours, when life is due to start again.

Milk/Bread/Celery/Tomatoes/Olive oil
Phone: Work
Hospital

When the kettle boils I make tea and stand sipping it in the hall. My old boarding-school trunk is in the cupboard above the boiler. I haul it out, blowing dust off the name and number I'd painted on the top before my first term – Beth Davis, Lower Fifth. No. 124. I unclasp the locks, and take out the tartan rug. I close my eyes and hold it to my face. It smells of safety.

In Ben's room the nightlight we brought from the States is glowing in the socket, an illuminated angel to bring him peace as he sleeps. His eyes are partly open, though vision-less, and although I've seen this phenomenon every night, this is the first time it has made my heart stop. I whisper his name, as I bend over him to brush his hair back from the warm forehead, and he takes a big breath and holds it for a second, then lets it out on a kitten cry. I push off shoes, jeans and cardigan, and gently slide under the covers with him, pulling the tartan rug across us both, tucking it in to hold us close. Sensing my presence, Ben turns on to his side so that I can spoon up next to him, as I used to do with his father. I slow my breathing to Ben's pace. When I curl around him and find his small hot hand, I place mine over it like the final piece of the jigsaw.

The Tale of the Cat Burglar and the Hair of the Dog

I'll say one good thing about divorce: once you've got used to it, in your subconscious self, you know where you are. For example, when you've been married twenty-five years, and you wake up to find a person stumbling around the bedroom in the pitch black you just say – Och for Goodness sake, Ian, if you want to stay up drinking Grouse till two in the morning with your so-called golfing-buddies, have the decency to pass out in the lounge instead of ruining my beauty sleep, thank you very much!! Whereas if you've been ten months divorced you're much more surprised and a wee bit cautious.

In actual fact, caution has always been my middle name, except for that time I found the receipts from the Aberdeen Holiday Inn in Ian's suit jacket, invoicing room 13 for dinner, bed and breakfast for two. (One of whom most certainly was not me, I should add.) Then, I threw caution to the winds, popped out to Butler and Wilson and got myself that whole Wallis Simpson replica set, then into that wee shoe place next door for a pair of gold silk mules with a matching bag, all on the joint Access account. Apart from that bittersweet day, I do tend to approach things antennae first.

So when I was woken by the tinkling of the Italian glass butterfly mobile above the bedroom window, I immediately thought, Oh yes? My guess was that it was Ian slipped back to ferret out the Fiorucci cuff-links or his gold Cross pen, which I'd tucked away with all his other trinkets in a box in the laundry room. He'd never think to look, he's allergic to soap. But it only took me a second to remember a) I'd changed the locks, and b) he's not the sort of man who would consort with criminals except in the line of duty. Ian would never break in. Financial Consultants are terribly law-abiding, in the main.

No, it wasn't long before the word burglar popped into my head. Strange, isn't it, how life echoes literature, because I'd just been reading a novel that came through the Book Club, about a burglar in New York who gets into terrible trouble, finding bodies in cupboards and so on. I did wonder if I was dreaming, but as soon as I started to pull myself up against the bed head I could feel my tennis elbow kicking in, so I knew I was wide awake.

Honestly, in all the years we lived in Dennistoun we never once encountered crime on a personal level, but the moment you get somewhere in life, acquire a few nice things, move into an executive property in the Merchant City, and sign your divorce papers, you're a target. I blame the media.

The Tale of the Cat Burglar

There have been so many features about the lifestyles of young film producers and advertising moguls and television personalities who live in this building – I mean if you wanted to steal a swanky laptop or a Scottish Bafta Award, this is where you'd come, because it's all laid out for you on a plate. We've got Him that produced *Braveheart* on one side and Her that presents the News on the other . . . And never mind the doorman, the alarms on the fire escapes, et cetera, anybody with a few O grades and a go-for-it personality would be through here like water through a sieve.

Anyway, there I was, in my high-necked peach satin nightie, reaching for the bedside light toggle, when all of a sudden this invader switched on a torch and shone it slap bang in my face. You watch these wildlife things with rabbits on motorways, but you never really understand why they freeze, until it happens to you. Looking back, of course, I should have worried in case there was a gun, or a knife, but since the only weapon I had, apart from my paperback, was my wits, that's what I used.

Go on, I said, go on, take whatever you want, I won't interfere. But I'm telling you now, there's nothing of any value in this house except my self-respect. I said, don't expect me to beg for my life, or have a wee cry, I'm not that sort of woman. I said, all my jewellery's fake except my engagement ring, and I sold that last September to pay off my daughter's University overdraft. You've picked the wrong flat, I said. And I folded my arms across my chest, and glared – well, squinted – into the light.

He was quiet all this time. Not a peep. I could just make him out standing by the dressing table, because the walls are white with 'hint of lilac', so's not to clash with the bed linen and the carpet. He looked a bit like Batman, just a dark figure, no visible features at all. Even semi-expecting it, I did get a shock when he moved slowly across the room to the foot of the bed and started fumbling about. I could hear a soft fabric sound, like top-quality towelling. Sure enough, as he came right up to me I could see he was holding the tie-belt from my Paloma Picasso robe that I got in the gift shop at Hamburg airport when I went with Ian to a seminar in 1995. He got a cushy expenses deal, so we'd enough for a matching pair, his burgundy, mine black, both with a silver moon and star motif on the back. His is still in the laundry room under the spare blankets.

Well, I shook my head. No, I said, that won't do. No, you can't use that. First, let me point out that it's very thick so it won't knot, if that's what you're planning, and second, as a gag, black deep-pile cotton would be the cruellest thing you could possibly use. I'd be retching in no time. I said, if you're serious about this, put your hand into the middle drawer of the cabinet here, and you'll find all my silk scarves, long ones rolled, square ones folded. There's a nice long plain green Jacquard, or a couple of Gucci ones, with the gem-stone designs on. Any of them will do, they all remind me of different holidays, so the psychological trauma might not be as bad as you'd think.

Well, he just stood there, while I was talking, with this black woolly thing covering his whole face, must have been terribly hot and prickly. And he made these funny noises, wee snorting sounds, halfway between a laugh and a cough, and then, he dropped the tie-belt and rushed toward the door to the 'en suite'! I thought, Aha! Big Mistake!, pushed back the duvet and was scrambling into my slippers when the next thing I heard, and you won't believe this, was the sound of vomiting. Vomiting, in my 'en suite', at 2.45am. Thank God it's fully tiled.

I've not been a mother all my life for nothing, and when I heard that noise I actually felt quite guilty. I've given him a fright, I thought, he's got a nervous tummy, and fear takes some people that way. A caring person can't ignore a guest up-chucking, you've got to offer them tissues and show them where you keep the Toilet Duck. So instead of running into the kitchen and dialling 999, I marched straight into the bathroom – and got the Biggest. Surprise. Of. My. Life.

The burglar was the dead spit of Michelle Pfeiffer. I swear to God. Michelle Pfeiffer with a Scottish complexion, though, if you can imagine that. The hair was bottle blonde, all electric from being under the balaclava, but everything else, the bee-stung lips, the big eyes, the wee black Cat-woman outfit, not PVC, just a pair of leggings and a polo neck . . . Gap, I think, it's what all the young ones wear. She was crouching there by the toilet, wiping her face on my hand-towel, a face white as a sheet, and from what I could see and smell she'd lost a tuna salad and a full bottle of chianti down my pan.

Oh Hell, she said, and I said, you can say that again. I said, right, m'dear, now, is there any more to come up? She shook her head, so I flushed the toilet, put the lid down, and hauled her on to the seat. Then I dampened the towel she'd been clutching and used it to wipe her face. I ran her a beaker of water and said Sip, don't gulp, and she took it and sipped. Then she cleared her throat and said Thanks.

Do you want some aspirin? I said. Or maybe a cup of tea? Some nice milky cocoa? The way she put her hand over her mouth at the mention of cocoa, I knew the only thing to give her was a hair of the dog. Come on, I said, we'll go into the lounge and have a wee chat and a brandy, and put the heating on. Come on.

In no time at all, Ian's Blue Label Courvoisier had her looking much less peaky. She sat on the sofa, and I sat in what used to be Ian's chair. I looked at her, and she looked at me. Well, I said, you'd better tell me everything.

Everybody remembers Olga Korbut and Nadia Coma-neci, the gymnasts who leaped about on those big rubber mats like wee angels. A far cry from what gym was like in my day. Anyway, Rona, my cat burglar, she'd been so inspired watching the Olympics she'd begged to do the training, and apparently did quite well until she was twelve and started getting too chesty. It's not sensible for a girl with a bosom to do somersaults all day, every day. So she took up jazz dancing to keep supple, went to University down south, got a degree in Anthropology, joined a graduate theatre group, learned to juggle and walk a tightrope, and all sorts of handy circus skills. Then she went to London, couldn't get a job with her degree, and fell in with a young man who said he was a property surveyor, but she discovered later on that he was in actual fact casing houses for a crack team of house burglars. Things soon went bad between them, and she came back to Glasgow, but within four months – this is a year ago now – both her parents had died. As if that wasn't tragedy enough, she was the only child, and left with a bungalow in Bearsden, which she had to sell below market value to pay for the funerals and death duties because Mum and Dad had let their insurance lapse.

I couldn't help thinking, when she was telling me this, that if only we'd met before I was divorced I could have got Ian to straighten things out for her, money-wise, but there you are.

Anyway, to cut a long story short, she tried everything, modelling, waitressing, being an extra in an Irn Bru advert, what have you, but it was no challenge to her, with all her skills. The more she talked and I listened, the more sympathy I felt. This is the sort of problem Tony Blair still needs to look at, but I won't talk about politics.

So. After all that honest toil, Margaret, she said, naturally I turned to crime. Shinning up drain pipes was the nearest I could get to living with primates in the lovely lovely trees. But I'm not really cut out for it. Every time I get my hands on someone else's property I think about Thatcherism, she said. We were halfway down the Courvoisier by that time. I said, how long have you been in the burglary business? Long enough to know better, she said, and I said, uh-huh, long enough to know you shouldn't drink when you're planning a night on the tiles, Rona. That's one thing that puzzles me, I said. In this book I'm reading, Bernie the burglar never touches alcohol before he goes out to work. Sober and silent, isn't that right? Oh she'd a great laugh at that.

It turned out the flat she'd intended breaking into was next door, Him that produced *Braveheart*. She'd been having a meal with a friend in a bistro where the film chap was a customer, and overheard him discussing a big flashy film party he was going on to, so she knew the coast would be clear till the crack of dawn. She'd read an article about him, and worked out which flat it was by the photo showing the roof-scape and his bonsai collection. But after finally getting rid of her friend at two in the morning, when she went up the fire escape she peeked in what she thought was his living room and spotted my daughter's Mel Gibson poster montage in the spare bedroom. Well, what with that and being a bit the worse for wine, she came through the wrong window.

We were both sitting there half cut, four in the morning by this time. I'd pushed Ian's chair into recline-mode, and Rona was stretched out across the suede sofa. I was so mellow, I never even told her to mind her Nikes on the leopard-print cushions. At some point we must both have fallen asleep, because I woke up with a pounding head, the sun streaming through the nets, and the smell of coffee floating out from the kitchen.

Well, I cancelled my wash and blow dry and we spent the morning together talking over the possibilities of turning the whole event into a screenplay. There's so much un-tapped potential in that girl, she just needs a bit of encour-agement. We thought we'd get Him Next Door to produce

129

it. Rona says she's halfway to an Equity card so she could play herself; and we'd make it a comedy with a happy ending. Which is not so far from the truth, really. Except for the glass butterflies on the mobile that got all tangled up, and the hangover from the Courvoisier, no harm was done, and we've come out of it as a team, with a sense of purpose.

Being burgled was the most positive thing that's happened to me since the divorce, and I couldn't be more delighted with the outcome. I can't wait to have a Bafta on the mantelpiece like everybugger else in this building.

GABE'S NOTES

I saw him first from the pavement. His feet approaching, knees bobbing at eye level. My blankets trailed on the ground, though they were not in his way. He hawked a gob of phlegm in my general direction – it missed, which made him scowl.

– Get outa ma fuckin' road, ya wee shite, he muttered, and rounded the corner into Rose Street, shoulders hunched. It was a dark night, about 7 o'clock on a damp Friday in November.

I made notes on his appearance, in particular of the eyes. The eyes are where it happens. His were brown, their shape narrow like his skull, with short lashes under strong brows. A brown iris that had no sparks of gold to it, no liquid depths. The man was thin and quite tall. He resembled a lurcher though in truth he had the fickle temperament of a fighting dog. The lines around the mouth were not kind ones. His hands were long, bony, stained and scarred. The tattoo on his neck was made by a ball-point pen and faded but still quite visibly a symbol of hatred, not least of himself.

I observed him next from the seat of a parked car. It was night again, an ordinary city-centre street. For a few flashing seconds I heard a harmonious cascade of music as he drank from a can, laughing with three others in a shop doorway, his arm round the shoulder of one of his companions. The music faded to dim cacophony when his knee rose and he pulled the man's face down on to it, punched his kidneys, kicked out at a second man. He backed off a pace. He leaned into an aggressive stance, enjoying it, looking for more. His fists were level with his hips, arms rigid, jaw thrust out. Steam rose from all their mouths as they shouted, blood dripped from the face of the wounded man, and Stuart laughed again. I watched him walk away, stiff legged.

This man, Stuart, is twenty-three. He's had the advantages common to his kind, a mother who loved him, an affectionate father who died before he could notice how much his son despised him. There was family, I noted, but he had abandoned them without cause. There was a child, a girl, but he disowned it, called the mother a whore, a fat cunt, a useless scheming lying fuckin' tart. The woman was wise enough to leave him. This man, Stuart, had the vocabulary of the streets from the age of fourteen, when he stole his first car.

On my third visit I saw him cry. December, another cold damp night. The bars were closing, and Stuart was the last to leave. He stood unsteadily on his feet, one hand to the wall. Vomit came up and out with little effort, spattered liquid on the cobbles. He spat a few times more and coughed, lit a cigarette. He walked the length of the street to the deserted bus station and put his head in his hands, sitting on a bench for a while. He reached for another cigarette but they were finished, and he crumpled the empty pack and tossed it into the gutter. He leaned back against the wall, folded his arms, closed his eyes. Eventually his mouth fell slack.

The place was quiet until around 1am. Four young men, younger than Stuart, woke him for sport, asked for money, picked a fight, and left him lying in his own blood and bile on the hard floor. He sobbed. The tears were not lesser tears than those of any man beaten, not cooler than those of the mother of his child, no less painful to cry than those of his own mother when he walked away from her. But they were only tears. His eyes became momentarily flooded with liquid which gave an illusion of humanity to his expression. I made a note of that.

The final occasion for assessment began while he walked through a park. It was January, the snow had fallen clean, grown grey with dirt, frozen hard, melted and frozen again. I watched him walk across the crisp white grass towards the Hospital. He was nursing his arm. The Accident and Emergency department was full of people with injuries caused by slipping on ice, crashing their cars, sprains, breaks, pain on most faces, and worry on the others. Stuart registered at the desk, filled in a form with bad humour, and took a seat between an elderly woman and a young man whose face was the colour of the snow. An hour passed, then another. Stuart had already smoked all the cigarettes he had left, standing by the doors, casting angry glances towards the blonde woman in charge of the waiting area.

The frail, elderly woman was seen and helped, and then the other man, hobbling on crutches. Soon Stuart's seat was at the centre of a large Asian family. One of their sons screamed so much he was taken into a cubicle straight away. Within three minutes Stuart's restlessness had risen to full anger. The nurses took the brunt of it, stoically and with skill, until a security guard intervened. The man was middle aged and heavy. He had spent the night standing in corridors, drinking tea and eating chocolate biscuits. His responses were slow. I watched as Stuart ignored his own injury to use his fists on the man's face, saw the withdrawal of life from the guard's eyes as he went down hard to the linoleum, heard the crack of his skull. I noted terror on the faces of the Asian children, drawn by the awful noise to witness violence. I saw a young doctor panic and run for the men's toilets to hide. I studied the eyes. Stuart's eyes did not change, though his face twisted in pain and fury, and he shouted:

– I've broken ma fuckin' arm, yah fuckin' cunts, ye!

Stuart ran out into the park, across the icy path on to the grass. He kept under the trees, sure of his pursuit, looking back, running on. He fell once and a moan escaped him as his arm jarred against the ground. He stuffed his hand into his pocket, cradled his elbow, and walked and jogged on, reached the main road, crossed it, ran panting up the darkest street and tried doors until he found a tenement stair open. He slumped down on the steps and his breath rasped like a blade sawing on hard timber. The ridge of his brows was furrowed, his mouth was open and ugly, and yet his eyes – his eyes were still just muddy, brown circles in a sallow mask of fear. He knew what he had done. There was no question of that. I made a note of it.

When he reached home he was disorientated. He put the kettle on the hob but couldn't find a match to light it. He spilled instant coffee from the jar which tipped, rolled, and smashed at his feet. He left the kitchen for the bedroom and drew the curtains. With his good arm he dragged a vinyl suitcase out of a cupboard and hauled clothes in fistfuls on to the cheap blue lining, then gazed down at the jumble for a moment as though frozen. Leaving the task unfinished, he pulled papers angrily out of drawers and searched the kitchen cabinets until he had found an address book, a brown envelope containing several £10 notes, a chrome-finished four-inch football trophy, two pairs of underpants, a personal stereo, a bottle of prescription tablets. These objects he put into the pockets of his jacket.

At last he was ready to leave. I saw him pause before opening the door, then switch off the light, and go down the steps two and three at a time. He paused again when he reached the street. Then he stepped out and walked briskly, head down, towards the bus station. Snow came drifting to fill the marks of his shoes, and settled on his hair. I followed him, recording his demeanour.

On the London-bound bus I sat beside him. His hand was stuffed through the buttons of his flannel shirt to support his damaged arm. Most of the night he sat with his brown eyes open, seeing nothing. At a motorway stop in the Midlands he left the bus and sat in the cafeteria, eating eggs and drinking a pot of strong tea, smoking cigarettes from the vending machine. Later, he found a truck going to Hull and hitched a lift with the driver, rebuffing the man's attempts at conversation with a few looks, a muttered word. The driver was glad to drop him at the outskirts of Hull. From the coast Stuart took a ferry to Ireland. I was next to him when the television news reported his name and a vague description, saying that he was wanted for questioning. There was no photograph yet. He heard his name and became still. His face showed nothing, but he dipped his head for a moment and it was almost a question. He drank a couple of double whiskies and claimed a seat as far away from children and noise as possible. But he knew I was with him now. Tears came to his eyes and pooled, dropped down his cheeks on to the flannel of his shirt. I counted them. He turned his head to look for me.

I didn't need to tell him it was over. I never do.

On deck, a light rain and a gusty wind kept passengers inside, but Stuart stood as far into the prow of the ship as he could get. He closed his eyes against the wet and opened them again, blinking, stood with his hands hanging at his sides. Then he placed one foot on the painted wire rail and stepped up. His jacket filled with wind and he put out his arms for balance, but he got caught at the last, and instead of a clean jump, he fell. The water rushed around us in a green swirl that bleached his skin, and bubbles fled from his mouth and nose.

The eyes looked straight at me. That's part of it. There's always a moment of acceptance. They want to know who has been watching to see them go. I could see that he had changed by the eyes. Not in colour, not the light in them. A new absence. An ending and a new start. It was recorded.

BARRY NORMAN'S TIE

Have you ever heard the expression 'barry' – as in fab, brilliant, really-really-nice? Like, 'that's a barry tie'? People I know used to say it all the time, not just about ties obviously. Anyway, it just came into my mind the other day, because I was watching Barry Norman, you know, the film guy on TV, and I noticed that he had on this really quite okay tie, which is unusual for him. Because, well, a) he usually wears these horrible patterned sweaters that older men think makes them look younger, b) when he does wear a tie, it's the colour of porridge, or something to do with cricket, and c) – I can't think what I was going to say for c).

A) and b) are probably enough. Oh, c) was about when he's
at Cannes, at night, and it's pouring with rain, and he's
wearing a velvet bow tie and shoving a microphone up
Arnold Schwarzenegger's nose.

Och, anyway, there he was one night wearing this actually quite nice tie, like it didn't shout at you, you know? It
was um, thingmy – discreet. It didn't get between him and
what he was saying about Bruce Willis. And I was so
amazed that I wrote and told him I liked his tie.

Veronica thought I was being a sap. She said I'd never get
a reply, but that's only because when she sent a fan letter to
Keanu Reeves, she just got this boring photograph of him
and his bare chest, with a sort of laser-printed squiggle in
the corner for an autograph. She tried to pretend she wasn't
disappointed, like she hadn't fantasised that he'd be calling
and asking her out and they'd fall-in-love-get-married-and-
live-in-a-five-bedroom-house-with-a-pool-in-Malibu, or something. But I could tell, and she's been sour grapes ever since
about me and Barry Norman. Because he *did* reply. On headed
notepaper. He said:

```
Dear Marina McLoughlin,
   Thank you for your very charming letter.
I have many ties, and I like all of them,
but I don't usually think about them, un-
less my wife or my producer tell me the one
I'm wearing has been irrevocably stained
by the product of BBC lunches. In this in-
stance, the tie was a recent birthday pre-
sent from my daughter, and I'm glad you
approve!
   I hope you keep watching the show,
Best wishes, Barrg Normaach.
```

Honestly, that's what his signature looked like it would
sound like if you said it, Barrg Normaach.

Anyway, I really like the way he wrote he was glad I approved, because he could have said, 'Listen, short arse, who cares what your opinion is?' Or not replied at all.

I was dead chuffed. I watched his next programme, which was on the same night I got his letter. And the moment he came on, I thought Oh NOOOOO!! Because he was wearing the most hideous tie in the whole entire world. It was totally mingin'. It looked like something you'd buy from Oxfam for 50p to wear to a seventies night. I could hardly bear to look at him, I was so shocked – you know, when your hero turns out to have feet of lead? How could he be so incontinent?

The next day, right, I just couldn't concentrate until I wrote to him again.

```
Dear Barry,
   Thanks a lot for your really very very
interesting letter. No offence or any-
thing though, but I watched the show last
night and I thought the tie you were wear-
ing was really -- sorry -- horrible. You
know the one, grey with orange and green
stripes, and you had on a beige shirt. Bar-
ry, you've got to do something about this.
```

And then I had this stupendous idea – so I added:

```
I've decided to make you a really brilli-
ant tie.
   Yours, etc., Marina.
```

And I sent it off.

Well, weeks passed, and I never got a reply, so I suppose I thought he must be offended. I watched the programme every week, plus the repeats, but he never wore the same tie twice, so I couldn't tell if maybe he'd taken my advice, or just liked the variety. Anyway, I started doing an evening course about then, in ceramics – you know, pottery? Pots?—and I got really absorbed in learning about slips and slabs and coil formations and stuff. Sounds a bit gynaecological, but it's good fun. I started making a big plate which came out really well, in the end. It's a kind of green. Nice curvy edges. I've seen things like it in galleries for pounds.

And then, out of the blue, I got a second letter from Barry Norman. It was very short.

```
Dear Marina,
   So; where's this tie, then?
   Yours, Barry Norman
```

– only this time it looked like Brryl Normo.

Well, first I made a photocopy of the letter, and sent it to Veronica, just for cheek; and then I pinned the original to the wall beside the dressing table, so's I wouldn't forget. And every morning, when I got up, I looked at it and thought about what kind of tie would really suit him. I held up bits of fabric, and thought about his colouring; beige, taupe, grey . . . mmm, that didn't help. I kept sneaking into my dad's room and looking in his cupboard, but he's only got the one tie he got married in, that he wears for funerals, apart from the British Rail tie he wears to work, so I was totally not inspired.

Then my ceramics course ended, and I started one in Spanish, and I think the letter must have fallen down the back of the mirror one day without my noticing, because I sort of forgot about it. My mind was crammed full of thoughts like how to pronounce 'chorizo', and where to buy it. Honestly, there's all these delicatessen counters in Safeway and Tesco, but they never ever have chorizo. Was it banned or something? These German foil-wrapped twiglet things are rubbish for paella. I'm sorry, but it's chorizo or nada.

Anyway, because of my Spanish course I had to go and see this film called *Jamón, Jamón*, which is Ham, Ham, in English, in fact. I don't know if you've ever been to Spain, but in the restaurants and cafés they have these hams hanging up from the ceiling, and it's dead unhygienic, cause there are flies walking all over them for years, and then they get sliced and put on your plate. I haven't actually been myself, but Veronica's dad did and he got food poisoning and had to go home, and threw up into his souvenir straw hat during take-off. Anyway, *Jamón, Jamón*, Ham, Ham, the film, Barry Norman had recommended it actually, and it was showing in this wee cinema – the kind where there's no ice cream or popcorn, but you can drink coffee – weird – and just before the film was about to come on, before the adverts, there was a symbol up on the screen; it was a piece of celluloid, film, you know, negative film, with I think they're called sprockets, down the side, and it was sort of curling around into a big 'S' shape, as part of the film company logo. My brain sort of went 'ping'. And that's when I knew what kind of tie to make Barry Norman.

As soon as I got home, I started rummaging about in the mending cupboard. My mum was watching *NYPD Blue*, and going on about how gorgeous that guy is, the one with red hair. I have to say our tastes are quite similar actually, and I got a bit distracted when he got into the shower with no clothes on, but eventually I found what I was looking for. An old white satin nightie I used for dressing up when I was about seven and thought I wanted to be an ice-dancer, except dramatic, like Margot Fonteyn as, maybe, Lady Macbeth, on Ice. With John Curry as Banquo's ghost.

Anyway, I got the scissors and cut it up until I had a big long strip of material, and then I got out the needle and thread and sewed it up the back, so it was half the size, and turned it inside out, and then put up the ironing board, and ironed it till it looked right. Kind of like a bendy white tape-measure. Then I found this indeligible marker pen that my mum used to use for my gym things, and I started drawing, black squares and wee black dots down the side.

It was rubbish. That was the word Veronica used, and I had to agree. So, I started again, and about three days and five versions later, I got it right. It actually looked incredible, the kind of thing you'd buy in a shop, or you'd see people wearing and go 'Wow, what a barry tie.' So I packed it carefully in tissue paper, and sent it recorded delivery. And waited.

Meanwhile, back at the High Chaparral, I finally found a place that sold chorizo. They also had all kinds of other Spanish and Mexican food, and I began to get really into it, especially the cactus salsa. Have you seen it? It's green. I wonder how they get the spines out? It's a bit scary at first, to think you're eating cactus, in case you get a spine in your throat and choke and have to go to hospital, like the Queen Mother and the fish. But it never happened. I started having cactus salsa with everything – on toast, with mince, and for a salad dressing. I got this book out the library about growing cacti and succulents – brilliant word that, succulents, makes you salivate, eh?—but eventually I realised I wasn't going to be able to grow enough prickly pears to make my own salsa unless I had a greenhouse, or I moved to Guadalajara. I even asked the guy at the hot house at the botanics, and we had this incredibly detailed conversation about mealy bug infestations and stuff, and how to grow from cuttings, and he asked me out. But that's another story . . .

Anyway, one day I came home from Spanish to find a BBC letter waiting for me. I made a cup of tea, and took it into my room, and settled down to read it – I was sure it was going to be a thank-you letter, and it was, but not quite what I'd expected.

```
Dear Marina McLoughlin,
  Thank you for your remarkable tie. It's
very clever, but you really ought to con-
sider the personality of the person
you're making it for. I never have and
never would wear a bootlace tie -- it's
just not my style. Thanks again.
  Best wishes, Brug Noord.
```

Honest – Brug Noord. Huh.

So. My first reaction was to feel a bit fed up. Then, really very very fed up. I thought about asking for the tie back, sending it to somebody else – but I don't think Mariella Frostup wears ties, she's quite feminine, and that *Moviewatch* guy is a complete banana. I didn't show the letter to Veronica, she'd just have gloated. I brooded. Yeah, I brooded. My mum was dead supportive and said she'd never liked Barry Norman anyway, and my dad just grunted something about Pearls Before Swine, cause he is a bit biblical, when he's in the mood. Eventually I realised I had to write back, get it out of my system, and stop being a martyr. I took my courage in both hands and picked up my biro:

```
Dear Brag Noodle,
  Thank you for your most interesting re-
ply. I'm sorry you didn't like the tie.
Unfortunately, my mum didn't have any
brown tweed or nauseating purple and yel-
low stripes in her scraps box, so I
couldn't make you the sort of tie you
usually wear. Anyway, they probably
wouldn't have been wide enough for you,
even if she had, as she's not got anything
kipper shaped.
  Yours most sincerely, Marina McLough-
lin.
  PS I would continue to watch your pro-
gramme if I thought you'd do something
```

```
about the way you comb your hair -- but who
am I to comment.
```

And I sent it off. The next time he was on TV, I sort of watched with a different eye, you know? Like, mentally arms akimbo. He wasn't wearing my tie. He wasn't wearing a tie at all, it was one of his kiddie-on Mondrian sweater days. And he had his legs crossed, and his beige trousers sort of pulled up a bit, and you could see his fawn sock and his white leg. Euch. My Uncle Ronald always sits like that, and it put me off. And I started to notice the bags under his eyes, and the way his hand sort of *sat* there on the arm of the chair, and then twitched, just when he made one of his witty comments. And I'm afraid even that began to annoy me. A bit like Clive James – you know how he can be so funny and then suddenly you go – wait a minute, that was really nasty, why did he say that? And I started thinking about these sacred golden calves, and how they're all older men, and how we look up to them and how really they're just insecure and bitter and cynical. A bit like Burt Lancaster in that film about Hollywood with Tony Curtis . . . *The Strong Smell* of Something, and they're both really young and good looking? So, maybe Barry Norman and Clive James are like Burt Lancaster in the story, they've seen so much corruption in Show Biz, they wouldn't recognise a gift horse if they looked it in the mouth?

Mind you, Burt Lancaster was totally brilliant. See when he was in that other film, with the helicopter on the beach, you know, in Scotland? That one, with Peter Capaldi doing his sparey voice? He was just like he was in *Bird Man of Alcatraz*, but older: but there was no bird. They had a mermaid, though, sort of. Anyway.

You know what? I bet Burt Lancaster would have liked my tie. He would have got the point. I mean it wasn't just A Tie, was it? It was a tribute. It was a gift horse. It was the gift horse of Troy.

The Broadway Theatre
Proudly Presents

ΔΟΝΠΤ ΣΙΤ ΥΝΔΕΡ ΤΗΕ ΧΗΕΡΡΨ ΤΗΡΕ ΩΙΤΗ ΑΝΨΟΝΕ ΕΛΣΕ ΒΥΤ ΜΕ
(NO NO NO . . .)

translated as

DON'T SIT UNDER THE CHERRY TREE WITH
ANYONE ELSE BUT ME
(NO NO NO . . .)

A Theatrical Entertainment In One Act
In The Style of Chekov & Hammerstein
(with additional dialogue by S. Freud)

*

Cast of Characters:
MASHA – a young woman who once met Julie Christie
KROPOTKIN – a young man who resembles Omar Sharif
APPLEBAUM – a fat geezer with a cigar, in the style of Burl Ives
MISHA – a small boy with a catapult
VARIOUS PEASANTS – various peasants

*

The action takes place in 1904 in a cherry orchard in a Soviet state where they
have a lot of cherry orchards, while the blossoms are falling. Peasants in quaint
regional costume wander about singing the Volga boat song, and watching as
events unfold.

*   *   *   *   *

(first production 1958)

147

THE ORCHARD: ENTER STAGE RIGHT, MASHA, A BEAUTIFUL YOUNG
WOMAN. SHE IS SOON FOLLOWED BY KROPOTKIN, A HANDSOME
YOUNG MAN.

MASHA (prettily)   The blossoms are falling, they are falling,
oh, how beautiful they are, look Kropotkin, the blossoms,
look . . .

KROPOTKIN (fervently)   I cannot see them, I have eyes only
for you, Masha my love, for your beautiful eyes, your
pale pale lips! How come your lips to be so full and yet
so pale? Ah, Masha, my darling girl, marry me, I beg
you! Now, before the trees are bare and the leaves are
brown . . .

PEASANTS (mournfully)   Before the leaves are brown, leaves
are brown . . .

MASHA (tearfully)   Stop, stop, Kropotkin, you know how it
breaks my heart to hear you beg . . .

KROPOTKIN (in miserable passion, kneeling)   I am nothing
before you, I am not worthy, I know it, but with your love
. . . I could . . . I promise, I could . . . change! I could
get therapy! We could work on our relationship . . . oh, I
do so want to be married before there's a revolution!

KROPOTKIN BURSTS INTO TEARS. MASHA COMFORTS HIM.
THE PEASANTS CLUSTER AND DRIFT IN THE BACKGROUND, A QUIET
MURMUR

ENTER APPLEBAUM, DRAGGING MISHA BY THE EAR

APPLEBAUM (pompously)   Aha! There you are, Missy! I have
a bone to pick with you! Not only do you allow your

illegitimate child to run riot through my property with his catapult, but now I find you in a compromising position with my nephew! Get up boy!

KROPOTKIN (pathetically)   Uncle Applebaum, I can expl . . .

APPLEBAUM (righteously)   Save it! This woman has encouraged you to stain your honour! Look at the knees of your uniform, why, you're a disgrace . . . as for you, Missy, I insist that you leave at once and take this monstrous infant with you . . .

MISHA (with spirit, wriggling)   He called me a little bastard, mother, so I shot him with my catapult when he was leaning out of the window of yonder castle . . . over yonder . . . look! See where the girls in wet blouses are gathering hay?

MASHA (furiously, to Applebaum)   Let him go, you brute! Oh, how could I ever have found you attractive! Misha, sweetheart, haven't I told you to be nice to 'Uncle' Applebaum? And as for you, (aside) don't you realise he's your own child, you fool? You must have noticed the way he smokes cigars? Don't you remember our long weekend in Kiev?

APPLEBAUM (spluttering)   Great jumping Jehosephat! Misha? MY Son!!!

PEASANTS (loudly)   Gasp! Goodness! Rhubarb, Beetroot, Borscht, etc . . .

KROPOTKIN (incredulously)   Masha, MISHA? MISHA, Masha?

PEASANTS (taking up the chant)   Misha! Masha! Misha! Masha! Misha! Masha! etc.

MASHA (scornfully)   Yeah, you always reminded me of my father – hey, maybe it was the cigar all along – eh! Phallic, Schmallic! What's the difference. . . .

LIGHTS DOWN TO BLACK

EPILOGUE

LIGHTS COME UP SLOWLY TO REVEAL KROPOTKIN HANGING BY HIS TIE FROM THE BRANCHES OF A CHERRY TREE. THE PEASANTS CUT HIM DOWN AND LAY HIM ON A PILE OF CHERRY BLOSSOMS, CROONING MYSTERIOUSLY, WHILST APPLEBAUM AND MISHA WALK OFF INTO THE DISTANCE TOGETHER, SMOKING CIGARS. STAGE CENTRE, MASHA DALLIES WITH A DASHING YOUNG POLICEMEN WHO LOOKS EVEN MORE LIKE OMAR SHARIF.

THE BITTER END